Dorrie Shelton and Mick Walters are on parallel journeys.

Dorrie stood studying the sign so intently that she never heard Mick approach her from behind. . . .

"That's one of the most interesting sayings I've ever read," Mick pointed out. "Before I begin my travels in the Whites, I always come here and read it. There's something mysterious about it."

Dorrie's eyes traveled to the profile of the Old Man's face and head formed from stone on the shoulder of the mountain. "Here in the mountains, God makes men. What do you suppose that means?"

"I've been trying to figure that one out for a long time," Mick admitted. . . . "Somehow these mountains change you. They do that physically, of course, because the trails are so demanding. But there must be more to these mountains—maybe a working of the spirit inside of man or something."

"I always love the mountains because they remind me of the power of God's creation," Dorrie remarked.

Mick flashed her a look of curiosity. "God's creation, huh? Guess you're a Christian then."

His observation sent her glancing back in his direction. "Yes, I am."

"I made a commitment like that once," Mick said, "but . . .God and I split and went our separate ways. . ."

LAURALEE BLISS is the author of nine adult Christian novels. Formerly from upstate New York, she now resides with her husband, Steve, and son, Joshua, near Charlottesville, Virginia, in the foothills of the Blue Ridge Mountains.

Mountaintop

Lauralee Bliss

Heartsong Presents

Thanks to the Appalachian Mountain Club in Boston, Massachusetts and especially to Sarah, who provided me with a vivid description of the Mount Washington area and the Lakes of the Clouds Hut. My love and thanks go also to my husband, Steve, who walked the trails in the White Mountains with me as well as took the plunge on the rock water slide at Franconia Falls.

A note from the author:
I love to hear from my readers! You may write to me at the following address: **Lauralee Bliss**
Author Relations
P.O. Box 719
Uhrichsville, OH 44683

ISBN 1-57748-246-8

MOUNTAINTOP

All of the characters and events in this book are fictitious. Any resemblance to actual persons, living or dead, or to actual events is purely coincidental.

Cover illustration by Victoria Lisi and Julius.

one

"Oh no, we're going to drown! Help!!"

Dorothea Shelton's eyes flew open. Outside a terrific noise could be heard pounding the fabric ceiling of the tent above her. A stiff wind rippled the blue material like the wind on the sail of a boat drifting out to sea. Dorothea rolled over to see her younger sister Gail wide-awake, clutching the puffy synthetic cover to her sleeping bag with clenched fists. Her eyes were wide in terror, her mouth poised to unleash another scream.

"Hey, it's going to be okay, Gail," Dorothea assured her sibling. "It's just a rain shower. The tent will keep us safe and dry."

Gail remained dubious of the tent's protection as her dark brown eyes surveyed the weak structure surrounding her. She scanned every nook and cranny of the seams for any water droplets that might have seeped through. "What if this thing leaks, Dorrie?"

"It isn't going to leak," Dorrie assured her. "I seam sealed it twice before we left home."

Gail's eyes blinked in confusion. "Seam sealed it? I don't get it. What does that mean?"

Dorrie stifled a chuckle over her sister's ignorance for the great outdoors, which she loved with a passion. "Remember when I set the tent up on the front lawn at home, I rolled on that stuff along the tent walls that you thought smelled like airplane glue?"

Gail's eyes rolled in remembrance and were accompanied by a wriggle of her nose. "Ugh, yes I do. The smell was awful."

"Well, that chemical was seam sealant. It's a special concoction that seals the seams of the tent and prevents water from bleeding through." Dorrie yawned once again, dismayed at having to explain to her younger sister the use of seam sealant at two in the morning. Her body ached for a few more hours of shut-eye. "So we're as snug as two bugs in a rug. Roll over and go back to sleep."

Dorrie sighed in relief to hear Gail rustle a bit inside her sleeping bag and plunk a head down on the feather pillow she insisted on bringing. Dorrie listened to the rain beating steadily on the roof of their makeshift home as she stretched her legs inside the cozy confines of her sleeping bag. With the scent of fresh rain seeping into the tent, she felt perfectly content.

Dorrie loved the great outdoors. She did not like the idea of having her civilized sister along on the trip—one who often argued for the comforts of a fancy hotel over a tent and who insisted on putting on her makeup every morning. Yet Dorrie resigned herself to putting up with her sister's idiosyncrasies, for she desired to rekindle a sibling relationship that seemed to have waned since her move to New York City over a year ago.

Since becoming a Christian herself, Dorrie wanted her sister to sample God's awesome creation while showing her the changed life of one devoted to the Savior. When Dorrie suggested a week-long vacation in the beautiful White Mountains of New Hampshire, where mountain scenery awaited them, along with the famous strip of outlet stores located in North Conway, Gail seemed genuinely intrigued.

"I'll go with you," her sister decided, "if you promise to stay a few nights in a motel instead of tenting every night and give me plenty of opportunities for shopping at the outlet stores."

Dorrie agreed to the ultimatum, but inwardly could not fathom how one might discover the intimate character of God scurrying by women who were in the crowded aisles of a store and who had arms ladened in shopping bags. Dorrie groaned at the thought of wasting precious days scouring aisles for clothes and shoes when she might be on a trail, ascending the steep mountainside to the summit, where a magnificent view awaited. From such a vantage point, high above the towns and farmlands, God seemed all the more real to Dorrie. She could relish in the magnificent work of the One who made the splendor of the heavens and the earth. If the view from a mountaintop was but a teasing look heavenward, where the Father dwelt, Dorrie knew heaven itself must be spectacular.

Dorrie sighed again. Forget such glimpses of the heavenly realms in the meantime. Shopping was a natural part of Gail's personality, so if Dorrie desired to renew their relationship and display the forbearance of a Christian, she would go along with shopping in the boring outlets. Doubtlessly a part of her would gaze in envy at the splendor of the Presidential mountain range looming before the store window.

The steady drumming of rain slowly died down to an occasional ping, ping on the tent fabric. Dorrie smiled to herself in anticipation of daybreak. There was nothing better than mornings after the rain, when every smell buried deep in the great earth would burst forth. The scent of flowers, mixed with the earthy odor of the soil would provide a perfect excuse for hitting one of the many trails in the area. Dorrie wondered if Gail was up to a climb today, but she doubted it after the conversation of the previous evening. Dorrie had scanned the map for hours by the golden glow of the propane lantern, tracing a beautiful route by a raging river that slowly ascended the shoulder of a great mountain and promised a startling view of the Presidential Range once they reached the summit. Gail sat at the picnic table, painstakingly removing her makeup when Dorrie shared in her idea of a hike.

"Not a hike already?" Gail had complained, immediately dashing Dorrie's hope for an adventure in the deep woods this early in the game. "I was hoping we might go to Franconia Notch and see that guy way up there on the mountain."

Dorrie stared at her sister, her eyebrows furrowing in

puzzlement. "What guy?"

Gail scrubbed her face with a washcloth. "You know, that guy carved out of stone."

"You mean the Old Man of the Mountain?"

"Yeah, the Old Man of the Mountain."

Dorrie sighed as she reverted her attention to the plastic-coated White Mountains hiking map, purchased in an outdoor shop before leaving on the trip. "Well, Gail, there'll be plenty of time for that. As long as the weather's this pleasant, we really should hit a trail. The views should be fantastic on the summit. . ." Dorrie heard the exasperated grumbling, accompanied by the bang of a fist striking the picnic table.

"Then you hike the trail and I'll go see the Old Man," Gail hotly informed her. "Look, Dorrie, I'm not going to spend my entire vacation hiking up and down some mountain, getting myself all filthy, achy, smelly, and for what? Some crazy view or something? Why, there's plenty to see right around here without having to hike a million miles. Like the Old Man."

Dorrie sensed the brewing altercation, something she desired to avoid at all costs on this trip. "Okay, we'll compromise. The first day you get to do what you want, then the next day I do what I want and vice versa."

Gail's eyes lit up. "Great!"

"The only condition to this is that I have reservations for the Lakes of the Clouds hut near Mount Washington at the end of the week. So you'll have to put up with a few days on the trail. The reservations are already set up and it's costing me a fortune."

Gail tossed the bucket of water in the woods, then proceeded to brush her teeth. "Just so long as I get in my shopping and my stay in the motel, like we agreed."

Right, Dorrie now thought to herself as she lay in her sleeping bag, listening to the sound of Gail's snoring. *The true outdoorswoman—with a purse full of money in one hand and a shopping bag in the other.* Dorrie flopped over on her foam sleeping pad, positioned herself more comfortably, and prayed for sleep to encompass her once more. As her eyelids grew heavy, she murmured, "Lord, help me get along with Gail. Help me be sensitive to her needs and show her the light of Christ on this trip. And please. . .allow me time to witness Your Creation on this trip besides the man-made creation of the shopping center. Amen." A frown tugged down the corners of her lips as Dorrie drifted off into a restless sleep and dreamt of an outlet mall spread out across the summit of her beloved Mount Washington.

ॐ

By morning the rain had dissipated, revealing a beautiful dawn and the clear, crisp air refreshed from the storm. Dorrie rose, stretched her extremities, and peeped out of the tent. Birds chirped merrily from treetops that formed a natural canopy of green over their campsite. "What a beautiful morning, Lord," she breathed. Excitement bubbled up for the adventures that lay ahead of her on such a glorious morning.

Next to her sleeping bag, Gail's bag was tossed in a bundle, denoting a young woman in an obvious rush to reach the rest room. Dorrie noticed her sister's makeup paraphernalia gone as well. She snickered, unzipped her sleeping bag, then searched around for her camp shoes. "Gail will be the beauty and I'll look like the beast," Dorrie murmured, forcing her feet into the narrow moccasins that seemed to have shrunk during the night. "She should save her makeup for special occasions, certainly not for the wilds of the Whites."

Dorrie emerged from the tent and once more stretched her hands upward to embrace the skies. Birds darted above her. Yellow and red wildflowers, reflecting the rays of the early morning sun, lent a brilliant color to the campsite. Dorrie hastened over to the rope where she had strung up a bag of food in a waterproof sack to protect the edibles from curious creatures during the night. She enjoyed practicing her outdoor skills whenever she had the opportunity, despite having the convenience of the car parked only a hundred yards away. As she untwisted the rope tied around a tree limb, she recalled Gail's panic at the thought of predators visiting their campsite at night.

"That's why I string up the food, Gail," Dorrie had explained, trying to alleviate her sister's jitters.

"I still don't see why you can't put the bag in the car instead of hanging it in a tree. Are you sure no animal can climb up and get that bag?"

"Not unless it has wings and can fly," Dorrie joked. "I've heard of flying squirrels, but a flying bear or raccoon are new ones to me."

Gail became angry at Dorrie's flippancy. "Don't tease me," she snapped. "I don't happen to like the idea of bears or other animals sniffing around the camp. I've heard of bears ripping tents and mauling people, Dorrie. It's no laughing matter. . ."

"Which is why I've strung up the food," Dorrie replied. "This is how hikers in the woods protect their supplies. It's worked for many, many years, so there's no need to worry."

Dorrie shook her head to clear her mind from the thought of last night's conversation. She grabbed hold of the rope and gently eased the foodstuffs to the ground just as a giggle materialized from the woods. Gail skipped along the campground road, all smiles as she swung the handle to the small carrying case containing her makeup. Dorrie noticed Gail's exuberant expression out of the corner of her eye and wondered what spawned the giddiness. *She looks like she's met the love of her life.*

"Oh, Dorrie, you won't believe it!" Gail breathed. "I just met the most gorgeous guy at the rest room."

Dorrie moaned in irritation. *There goes the great plan for a sisterly reunion. She still hasn't let go of her boy craziness from her high school years.* "That's a cozy place to meet. . .

the rest room," Dorrie remarked with a hint of sarcasm, fumbling to undo the knot securing the food bag. She thrust a hand inside, retrieving granola bars and orange drink mix.

"I told him we were going to visit the Old Man up there in the mountain. He laughed and said that's where he's going, too."

Great, Dorrie thought again, suppressing her irritation as she strode over to the picnic table to retrieve a plastic container with which to mix up a batch of Tang. *Just what this trip needs. . .two lovebirds twirling around the White Mountains.* Dorrie sighed in frustration before silently murmuring a prayer for patience and long-suffering—the two characteristics she sadly lacked at that moment in time. With great difficulty, she asked, "So you plan on meeting him at the Old Man? What time?"

Gail shrugged before disappearing into the tent. "I don't know" came her muffled reply. "He wasn't sure when he'd be going. He says he must stop at the hiker's information booth and check on the condition of a trail he wants to hike."

Dorrie's ears pricked in interest, intrigued by the idea of a fellow outdoorsman interested in hiking. Her hand ceased shaking the container. "He's a hiker, huh?"

Gail emerged from the tent, combing out snarls from her curly hair. "Yup. He says he comes to these mountains every summer because he loves to hike in this area." Gail threw the comb into the tent before venturing over to the picnic table, plopping down, and sliding her legs underneath. She picked up the granola breakfast laid out for her. Her mouth opened, ready to sink her teeth into the crisp, spicy bar.

"Hold on, now, we have to pray," Dorrie reminded her sister, taking her place on the bench opposite her.

Gail dutifully bowed her head and closed her eyes while Dorrie offered up prayers of thanks for the beautiful day, for their safety during the rainstorm, and for the adventures that lay ahead. "And thank you, Lord, for this food. In Jesus' name,

Amen." Dorrie picked up her tin cup and toasted her sister.

Gail made a face. "I thought we'd be sitting here all day listening to that prayer of yours."

Dorrie opened her mouth, poised to deliver a special monologue she had rehearsed on the importance of knowing Jesus as a personal Savior, then decided it might be ill-timed when she saw the look of disgust emanating from her sister's face. Dorrie recalled the day when she gave her own heart to the Lord and the wonderful feeling of having a close relationship with her Savior.

When she first told Gail of her newfound beliefs awhile back, her sister only wriggled her face and blatantly informed Dorrie not to become religious around her. "I don't need God to run my life. Things are going great right now."

Great to Gail meant having fun with her friends, frequent dates with guys who came calling, or shopping for a new outfit at the nearby mall. Fun for Dorrie meant spending time listening to contemporary Christian music, attending various revival meetings at church, or taking long walks in the outdoors that beautifully displayed God's creative touch.

With Gail's continued interest in the dating scene, Dorrie reflected on her own commitment in that area. Despite the insistence by coworkers that she date, Dorrie committed herself to living a single life for the Lord. She did not want the heartache associated with dating unless she was certain this was the man she intended to marry. Watching the pain and misery that ensued after Gail broke up with her boyfriend of nearly two years, Dorrie tried convincing Gail to change her outlook in the dating arena. "Let God be the matchmaker," Dorrie suggested to her sister. "That way, you won't get hurt."

Gail pointedly told Dorrie she was off her noodle, then rushed out to find another guy to cover up the pain of the broken relationship. Dorrie only offered her sister to the Lord, praying on a daily basis for her salvation. She hoped this trip to the mountains might somehow stimulate her sister's appetite to know God.

"So what's this guy's name?" Dorrie wondered, now changing the subject as she bit into her granola bar.

Gail cupped a hand to her mouth. "Wouldn't you know it. I didn't even ask him his name. Oh well, I'm sure I can't miss him in a crowd. He's absolutely gorgeous, Dorrie! Blue eyes, blond hair, and a gorgeous set of muscles."

"Humph," Dorrie mumbled. She sat sipping her tin cup filled with Tang while savoring the beauty of the forests, wishing her sister would take a little more interest in the creation surrounding them and not the creation of men.

"He looks like one of those guys who lifeguards at the beach every summer," Gail went on dreamily, closing her eyes as she reminisced. "Tanned, a superb build. . .oh, he's the perfect image of a male model."

"Well, I wouldn't get yourself all excited about Mister Wonderful. You'll probably never see him again with all the tourists and hikers around."

Gail sat upright and finished her breakfast. "Well, I'm sure gonna try. If not, then I can still dream about him." She cupped a chin in one hand and closed her eyes.

Dorrie snorted softly as she arose from the table, rinsed out her cup, then assembled the necessities she would need inside her daypack: maps, guidebooks, water bottle, first aid kit, and a few extra granola bars. Opening her eyes to observe Dorrie with the pack open on the picnic table, Gail rose and threw in her own possessions for the day: comb, mirror, lipstick, and perfume.

"You shouldn't wear perfume out in the woods, Gail."

"Why not? I happen to like this scent very much."

"It'll attract every stinging insect from here to Maine. You know, there are many varieties of insects drawn to a host by their scent, so. . ."

Gail interrupted the explanation by suddenly ripping the pack from Dorrie's possession, stuffing a hand inside, and withdrawing her favorite bottle of perfume. "There, you satisfied?" she barked. "Honestly, Dorrie, all you can do this morning is find fault with everything." She twirled the bottle of perfume in her fingers, then studied the label before adding with a hint of sarcasm, "Is that what you call being a good Christian?"

Dorrie opened her mouth, ready to issue a stiff retort, then thought better of it. After a quick analysis of the morning's events, she realized she had been quite nitpicky with her sister, who was not accustomed to the rigors of outdoor living. "You're right, I have been rather bossy," she admitted, much to Gail's surprise. "I just don't want you getting all bit up and having a miserable time."

Gail's anger quickly abated. A grateful smile now filled her delicate features. "Thanks for the concern, Dorrie, but I'm willing to take the risk." She deposited the perfume inside the confines of the pack. "I don't plan on smelling like an animal sitting in a manure pile. Disgusting."

Again Dorrie sensed the overwhelming urge as an older sibling to inform Gail she'd regret her actions, but she bit down hard on her lower lip to stifle the words. "Look. . .how 'bout we call this a cease-fire, if it's all right by you?" Dorrie suggested instead. "We're supposed to be renewing a relationship here, not climbing over each other's back. What do you say?"

"That's fine by me," Gail agreed. "Cease-fire."

❧

The two young women jumped into Dorrie's car, preparing to head to the main highway in search of the Old Man of the Mountain. On their way out of Lafayette Campground, where they had spent the night, they passed a small outbuilding on the left with detailed maps of the White Mountains plastered along the outside walls. Studying them intently was a tall, muscular man with a bandanna wrapped around his head and clad in a tank top. When Gail saw him, she squealed with a noise that forced Dorrie to slam on the brake in a hurry. "Would you look at that? There he is! That's him! That's the guy I met at the rest room!"

Dorrie followed her sister's eager finger, examining the profile of the man who stood with a pack resting against his ankles. He studied a map held in one hand, then raised his eyes to compare it with the one fastened to the wall of the building. While Gail sat goggle-eyed over the man, Dorrie admired the pack he owned—an expensive internal frame pack, probably a three-hundred-dollar model by the storage capacity. He appeared ready for a month-long adventure with various accouterments strung into loops and hooks on the pack itself and a foam sleeping pad rolled up neatly and fastened to the top. Dorrie inhaled a deep breath, wondering what sort of adventure he planned to embark on.

Gail fumbled for the latch to the car and leaped out. "Hey! Hey!" she called out, waving her hand.

Dorrie sat motionless in the front seat as her sister ran up to the man and engaged him in a noisy dialogue. Her fingers tapped the steering wheel, watching her sister's face light up with the rows of even, white teeth smiling at the stranger. "C'mon Gail," she murmured. "We didn't drive all the way up here just to have you fall for some guy you'll never see again in your life." Again Dorrie fought to suppress the impatient urges within her before they exploded into something she would later regret.

Several minutes passed by as Gail chattered on. From the smile parked on the guy's tanned face, he appeared quite amused by her winsome ways. He pointed at the map, then at his pack, explaining his intent. Gail nodded and began side-stepping her way back toward the car.

"Well, okay. . .maybe this afternoon, then," Gail called out to him over her shoulder before parading triumphantly back to the car. She exhaled a loud sigh as she slid into the passenger's seat. "Oooh, what a dreamboat!"

"So what's the dreamboat doing? Sailing the seven seas?"

"Mick's planning a quick hike up the Appalachian Trail across the road over there. He wants to test out his new pack for fit and weight."

"The Appalachian Trail, eh?" Dorrie glanced out the car window, thinking of one of her life's goals—to hike the entire two-thousand-mile distance on the famed foot trail stretching from the state of Georgia all the way to Maine. Of course her coworkers and her family only laughed at such an idea, yet this did not deter Dorrie. Often she would visit the state park near her parents' home and walk portions of the famed trail, marked by the standard white blazes painted on the trees. She imagined herself tackling the infamous trail in one six-month adventure with a pack on her back and a hiking staff in one hand.

Gail's voice now interrupted her contemplations. "Mick says he's going to see the Old Man this afternoon, Dorrie, so if you want to do something else this morning, that'll be fine with me. In fact, I'll even take a hike with you or something."

"Yeah, sure," Dorrie muttered under her breath, starting the ignition. *Of course, now that the dreamboat hiker is in the picture, she's ready to tackle the trail. Why wasn't she this animated when I wanted to go hiking?* Dorrie glanced at her rearview mirror in time to see the man named Mick shrug on his pack and adjust the wide hip belt encircling his narrow waist. A pang of envy bit her, wishing she might have a pack on her back ready to attack the famous Appalachian Trail. "He's one lucky dog," she whispered.

"What was that?"

"Nothing," Dorrie answered. Her foot moved to the accelerator. "C'mon, it's too late to start on any decent hike now. Guess we might as well spend money and see the Flume or whatever that water gorge is they advertise around here."

two

After a bite to eat in the snack bar at the Flume, Dorrie pulled into the parking lot for the natural rock formation called the Old Man of the Mountain. Tourists young and old ambled their way down the paved trails to the various observation points. Gail bounced up and down with more excitement than usual, her eyes carefully scanning every face for the one belonging to Mick. Ignoring her sister's zeal, Dorrie grabbed her camera from the glove compartment of the car and followed the hordes of people making their way to see New Hampshire's most famous natural landmark.

"I wonder if Mick made it back from his hike?" Gail asked, glancing around as they sauntered down the trail.

Irritated at Gail's continual preoccupation with the unknown man, Dorrie retorted, "Well, I wouldn't suffer heart palpitations worrying about it. If you see him, then you'll know he didn't get lost on the trail."

Gail frowned at her sister's snippy remarks. "You're jealous 'cause I saw him first."

Dorrie widened her eyes and laughed outright. "Believe me, I am *not* jealous. I have more important things to do in my life than track down some weird guy."

"Yeah, but he's a hiker, Dorrie, just like you," Gail pressed. "Didn't you see all his gear? Why, you must be a little interested to learn more about him. Huh?"

Dorrie twirled a forefinger around in midair.

"You're too much," Gail said with a short chortle of her own.

They soon arrived at the circular platform overlooking a

pristine lake that reflected the tiny image of a grizzly stone face carved into the mountainside. Dorrie snapped pictures while Gail took up one of the large telescopic viewers for rent, eager to examine the formation close up. She deposited the necessary change, then leaned one eye into the lens. "Hey, Dorrie, you should see this! Why, the rocks really do look like an old man, how about that?" She scrutinized the images for a minute longer. "Hey, it also looks like someone had to wire up all the rocks so they wouldn't fall apart."

Dorrie snapped her last picture, then went over to take a look. "Yup, they sure did," she confirmed as she stared intently through the lens of the viewer, noting every detail of the famous rock formation—from the bearded chin to the crop of stony hair. The face of the man stared forward as if thoughtfully perusing his bird's-eye view far above the rest of creation. "Bet the view is fascinating from up there," Dorrie commented, wishing she might join the Old Man in his gaze of the world around him. "I wonder if people are allowed to climb that mountain for a closer look at the formation?" Dorrie glanced up from the viewer for Gail's reaction, but found her nowhere in the immediate vicinity. Embarrassed by the idea she had been conversing with herself all this time, Dorrie muttered, "Great, now where did she run off to? Honestly, it's like trying to keep an eye on some kid."

A familiar giggle alerted Dorrie to her sister's whereabouts. She noticed Gail striding up the pathway, clinging onto the arm of the man called Mick, who ascended the walkway effortlessly with a set of muscular legs and feet clad in sandals. A pair of binoculars swung over one broad shoulder. He wore a red bandanna around his forehead with spikes of straw-colored hair poking out underneath.

"Hey, Dorrie!" Gail called out, grinning from ear to ear. "Here he is! This is Mick."

"Hi," Mick greeted, displaying a bright smile of white teeth that stood out in sharp contrast to his tanned skin.

"Hi," Dorrie answered pleasantly. "So, did you enjoy your hike on the A.T.?"

Mick seemed taken aback by her question. "What? The Appalachian Trail? Uh, yeah, I did. How did you know about the hike on the Trail?" When Dorrie pointed out her sister as the chief informant, Mick nodded his head in comprehension. "Oh, I see. Guess Gail told you my plan."

Dorrie nodded.

"And you are?"

Gail pushed her hand against Mick's strong chest in a gesture of embarrassment. "Oh, I'm sorry, Mick. I totally forgot to introduce you two. This is my sister Dorrie."

"Dorrie," he repeated, sizing her up with a swift eye.

"It's short for Dorothea," Gail went on. "Mother decided to name her after a famous nurse during the Civil War, Dorothea Dix. She was a big history buff back then, which probably had to do with her younger brother—my Uncle Bob, who's involved in all that Civil War reenacting. She had a choice between Dorothea or Clara, for Clara Barton. Isn't that cute?"

Dorrie blushed deep red. Inside she fumed *Thanks a lot for sharing all the family secrets, Miss Quick-with-the-Tongue*.

Mick's grin grew wider as his blue eyes surveyed Dorrie in amusement. "That *is* cute."

Dorrie could see this conversation was going nowhere but downhill and decided to make a fast exit before Gail divulged other stories from their past. "Well, I'm going off to do a little exploring. See you two later."

"Nice meeting you, Dorrie," Mick said congenially, holding out his hand.

Dorrie accepted the hand he offered, surprised by the strength and warmth imparted in the handshake. Wheeling about on one foot, Dorrie continued on down the trail with Gail's silly giggle echoing on the wind that ruffled her hair. "I can't believe she embarrassed me in front of the hotshot hiker," Dorrie complained. "The two of them deserve each other. God, it's just going to be You and me today."

The path led Dorrie by some pretty wildflowers and along a lazy, winding stream that boasted a variety of minnows and other small fish. As Dorrie examined the flora close up, she wished she had brought along a manual identifying the various wildflowers of New England. Bees buzzed to and fro among the assortment of flowery heads, eager to sip up the juicy nectar. All at once, Dorrie remembered Gail's perfume and wondered if she had been attacked by the bugs yet. "What a girl," Dorrie remarked, thinking of Gail's performance up until that point. "Heaven knows why we agreed to do this together. Here I planned for us to renew some type of relationship after a year of noncommunication, only to have this guy plop down right in the middle of it. . . ."

Dorrie sighed and sat in a pretty spot beside the body of water called Profile Lake, which glistened beneath the rocky formation of the Old Man of the Mountain. Here she soaked in the peace and tranquility of an area totally devoid of the busy life she left in New York as a secretary for a business firm. In these pristine surroundings, she could enjoy the beauty and ease the tensions prevailing throughout her body from the mounds of work she was forced to do for her boss.

Dorrie sat for a time, then scooted herself closer toward the bank of the lake, peering at her reflection in the crystal-clear waters. Chocolate brown eyes like all those in her family stared back at her. She shook her short, dark brown, bobbed hair that came just past her earlobes—a cool hairstyle she preferred to wear in the summer. Her mother disliked the cut, saying she looked too much like a man. Gail, on the other hand, possessed the "beautiful, naturally curly hair of a grand lady," Mother remarked to her friends, proudly showing off her youngest daughter. Dorrie would not admit her younger sister was the favorite, but Mother's words definitely substantiated the high ranking Gail held in the family. The activities they shared provided more clues. Mother shopped with Gail, Mother went out to luncheons with Gail, Mother giggled like Gail over some silly thing. . .the list went on and on.

Dorrie picked up a stick and traced a path through the waters, silencing a bitter wave of jealousy that crept up within her. Perhaps Mother did prefer Gail to her, but Dorrie should not feel any lack for she had God, a Father in heaven who loved her. Dorrie pitched the stick into the middle of the lake and rose to her feet, preparing to venture back to the observation platform.

She arrived to find Mick and Gail sitting side by side on a bench, sharing a double-dipped ice cream cone from the concession stand. Gail waved at her. "Hi, Dorrie! Wanna bite?"

"No thanks," Dorrie said.

Mick wiped off his mouth on a napkin he held in one hand, then inquired if she would like a cone.

Dorrie smiled and shook her head, conscious of his blue eyes resting on hers for several moments. "No, no thanks."

Gail noticed the silent interaction, too, for she thrust the cone once more in his face, successfully disrupting the contact. "Here, Mick, your turn." As he licked the cone, she snuggled up next to his arm and turned her attention toward Dorrie. "Didn't I tell you Mick looked just like a lifeguard, Dorrie? And guess what? During the summers he watches the young kids at the neighborhood pool where he lives. That's where he gets his fabulous tan."

"That's nice," Dorrie remarked.

Mick shrugged sheepishly, returning the treat to an eager Gail, who bit down on the sugar cone with a satisfying "mm." "Yeah, it earns me a little extra money in the summer."

"What do you do the rest of the time," Dorrie wondered, "besides lifeguard duty and rambles in the woods?"

Mick glanced at her and smirked. "So you could tell I enjoy my hikes."

"Well, it didn't take much to figure out with that fancy pack of yours."

"The pack's a present to myself," he admitted. "Anyway, I teach science at the middle school near where I live."

Gail screwed up her face. "You mean like biology?"

Mick nodded. "That's it exactly."

"Ugg, I'll never forget seventh-grade biology, when we had to dissect those disgusting frogs and worms on those black, greasy dissecting trays." Gail clutched her stomach, feigning nausea. "And the smell of formaldehyde nearly made me sick to my stomach."

"Well, the preservation process is odorless now," Mick told her. "Guess too many people complained about the foul smell."

"I rather enjoyed biology myself," Dorrie interjected, her eyes focusing once more on the stony image of the Old Man perched high above her. "The frog was fascinating. I remember one of my classmates discovering these tiny black eggs inside one of the frogs."

Mick straightened with interest. "The frogs do provide the students with an excellent opportunity to observe the internal organs of a living organism." He went on to explain several incidences in his class where he assisted the more squeamish students with their dissecting procedure and the various discoveries that were made.

Gail noticed Mick's attention drifting toward Dorrie and once more she used the ice cream cone as a diversionary tactic. "Mick, can you finish the rest of this? It's starting to melt."

Mick obliged, taking bites of the cone while continuing to entertain Dorrie with his stories, much to Gail's dismay. Finally Gail uttered a loud yawn and rose to her feet. "Well,

I'm bushed. I think we should call it a day."

Mick threw the napkins into a nearby trash receptacle. "You ready to go?" he asked Dorrie.

She nodded, glancing once more at the scenery before following the pair back down the paved path. Just beyond the platform, a wooden sign erected near a lookout point for the Old Man caught Dorrie's eye. She paused before it, reading the lines twice while allowing the message to sink deep into her soul.

> *Men hang out their signs indicative of their respec-*
> *tive trades.*
> *Shoemakers hang out a gigantic shoe;*
> *Jewelers a monster watch;*
> *And a dentist hangs out a gold tooth;*
> *But up in the mountains of New Hampshire*
> *God Almighty has hung out a sign to show*
> *That there, He makes men.*
> *Attributed to Daniel Webster*

Dorrie stood studying the sign so intently, she never heard Mick approach her from behind and peer over her shoulder. His resonant voice in her ear made her jump. "That's one of the most interesting sayings I've ever read," Mick pointed out. "Before I begin my travels in the Whites, I always come here and read it. There's something mysterious about it. . ."

Dorrie's eyes traveled to the profile of the Old Man's face and head etched in stone on the shoulder of the mountain. "Here in the mountains, God makes men. What do you suppose that means?"

"I've been trying to figure that one out for a long time," Mick admitted, scuffing the toe of his sandal across the pavement. His gaze followed hers across the breadth of the mountain looming before them. "Somehow these mountains change you. They do that physically, of course, because the trails are so demanding. But there must be more to these mountains— maybe a working of the spirit inside of man or something."

"I always love the mountains because they remind me of the power of God's creation," Dorrie remarked.

Mick flashed her a look of curiosity. "God's creation, huh? Guess you're a Christian then."

His observation sent her glancing back in his direction. "Yes, I am."

"I made a commitment like that once," Mick said slowly, "but along the way, God and I split and went our separate ways. I couldn't believe He would allow such terrible things to happen. It had to do with. . ."

"There you are!" Gail's voice shrilled as she came up to them, silencing Mick. "I was wondering where you slipped away. C'mon, it's getting late." She took up Mick's hand, urging him on.

Dorrie followed behind, curious as to what Mick was ready to confess before Gail interrupted. Once in the parking lot, Gail gushed over Mick, telling him what a wonderful afternoon it was. "Oh, I had such a great time, didn't you, Mick? I think it's great we just happened to meet like this only to find out we enjoy doing the same things." She went on without drawing a breath. "So, what are your plans in the morning? We're staying at Lafayette Campground again tonight in our tent, site thirty-three, if I'm not mistaken. You take a right when you enter the campgrounds. It's not that far in from the main entrance actually. You should see our campsite, Mick. It's really a nice place, even though I'm afraid some animal might come in the middle of the night and rip open our tent. I've heard about such things, you know, like those terrible grizzly attacks in Alaska and the people who were mauled."

"Well, there are no grizzlies in these mountains, Gail," Mick managed to say before Gail continued to ramble on about her need for protection and how the mountains sometimes frightened her.

Increasingly vexed by her sister's flirtations, Dorrie finally grabbed Gail by the arm and propelled her toward the car. Gail was reluctant to leave, as her feet scuffed the pavement like a child being pulled off a favorite slide at the playground. "Well, good-bye, Mick!" she said cheerily, waving as he retreated to his own vehicle. Gail sighed as she opened the door to the passenger's seat. "I sure hope I see him again. Isn't he absolutely divine, Dorrie?"

"Well, I wouldn't say he's divine, but, yeah, he is a nice guy."

This comment triggered a raised eyebrow from Gail. "Well just remember, big sister, I saw him first. He's mine."

"Mick isn't a toy bear you can carry around with you everywhere you go," Dorrie retorted. "I have a feeling the man's been through a rough time in his life. And quite frankly, I'm kind of curious to know what it was."

Gail blinked thoughtfully. "What makes you say that?"

Dorrie steered the car around, approaching the on-ramp for the Franconia Notch Parkway, which would return them to their tent site at Lafayette Campground. "Oh, just some comments he made, or tried to make. Nothing for you to worry about."

Gail crossed her arms, intent on the view out her window. "Well, I will worry about it, Dorrie, if you're taking any interest at all in *my* man."

Dorrie rolled her eyes. "Gail, I already told you earlier, as far as I'm concerned, you can have the dude all to yourself. I'm not looking for any relationship except for the one I'm attempting to foster with you. . .which we're quite unsuccessful with right now."

Gail remained in her agitated posture and refused to acknowledge her sister. Dorrie knew her words meant little, for she could detect the jealousy and resentment in Gail's facial expressions. How could she convince Gail that she was much more interested in family ties than some strange man?

Gail said little as they prepared their evening meal over the two-burner propane stove, then washed up the tin plates and cups and allowed them to air dry on the picnic table. The evening was picture perfect, with stars glinting between the tree branches that swayed in the breeze. A crescent moon rose in the night sky, bathing the campsite in an incandescent light. Dorrie studied her sister's brooding, wondering what she might say to lighten up the evening. She lit the propane lantern and withdrew her Bible from a stack of belongings. When Gail saw the leather book, she grumbled a few words about hypocrisy and the foolishness of pious living, then grabbed the flashlight and declared she was retiring early.

"Before you go running off, Gail, we need to settle this once and for all," Dorrie said slowly.

Gail shook her head. "I know you. You'll just tell me off and ram Bible verses down my throat."

"No, I won't."

Gail fumbled with the on and off switch to the flashlight, watching the ground illuminate under the yellow beam of light.

"I think it's downright silly getting all uptight over a guy you happen to meet at the rest room," Dorrie went on. "We're here to have fun, Gail, not pick fights. Let's just give it a rest, huh?"

Gal shrugged her shoulders.

"C'mon now, don't let the sun go down on your anger, and already the sun's been down an hour."

Gail flashed Dorrie a look of irritation. "Sounds like a saying from that Bible of yours or something."

"Gail, I only want us to have a good time, okay?"

Gail flashed her a look. "Then if you really want to make me happy, let's go outlet shopping tomorrow. I'm tired of all this camping in the woods."

Dorrie hesitated until the mask of irritation filtered across the face of her sister. "All right, we'll drive on down the Kancamagus Highway tomorrow and see what kinds of outlet stores are in North Conway. I can handle that." She added silently, *So long as we can both put that man named Mick out of the picture and go on with our vacation.*

Gail's face brightened at the suggestion, accompanied by a smile. "Now that sounds like fun."

Dorrie sighed in relief before offering Gail good night, then returned to her Bible study. "Thank you, Lord," she murmured. "I know Your Word says to live peaceably with all men, but Gail is certainly a challenge. I only hope we can continue to avoid these flair-ups of ours while we're on vacation." Dorrie paused, watching several white moths flutter around, attracted by the yellowish glow generated by the mantles of the propane lantern. "Gail needs to be like that," she sighed, returning her attention to the Word lying open before her. "She needs to hover around You, Lord, the light of the world."

three

The next morning, Dorrie stood in front of the propane stove heating water for the breakfast oatmeal, when she heard a cheery whistle and a deep voice offering a pleasant good morning. Startled by these masculine sounds, she snapped up her head at the surprise visitor to their campsite—the tall form of Mick clad in shorts and a T-shirt.

"Well, I did find it," he complimented himself, gazing around their camp. "Nice isolated spot you've got here."

Dorrie stood speechless and dropped her face so her eyes encompassed the pot of water and the bubbles that had just begun to rise to the surface.

"Where's Gail?"

Dorrie turned off the flame, then added the oatmeal mix. "At your favorite stomping ground."

Mick stared at Dorrie quizzically. "What favorite stomping ground?"

"The rest room."

Mick remained puzzled until the comment registered, then a slow smile spread across his face. "Oh, I get it. . .the place where we first met." He spanned the seating area to the picnic table with his muscular legs. "So what's cooking?"

Dorrie whirled the concoction around with a small spoon. "Oatmeal. You're welcome to have some."

"I might snag a bite, thanks. Guys don't cook too well for themselves. I usually survive on power bars when I'm out in the wild."

"Don't you get tired of the same old thing?"

Mick nodded. "Sure. That's why I hit the town restaurants

whenever I can. I know every good eating spot in the Whites. Name the town and I'll tell you where to eat."

"North Conway," Dorrie said.

Mick cocked his head, eyeing her in both amusement and curiosity. "Is that a serious question or are you cracking jokes again?"

Dorrie rested her eyes once more on his and noticed they were pale blue to match the morning sky. His honey blond hair appeared unusually brilliant when touched by the rays of the sun. "No, I'm serious. Gail and I plan on driving down the Kancamagus Highway. I promised her we'd visit the outlets in North Conway today."

"Outlet shopping, eh? Too bad. There's some real scenic spots off the highway. Great places to swim, too. In fact, there's a favorite place of mine, Franconia Falls, which has a natural rock water slide."

Intrigued by this description, Dorrie ceased stirring the oatmeal and stared at him wide-eyed. "Really? That sounds great!"

"Yeah, it's right next to a walk-in campsite, Franconia Brook, I think it's called. There're nice platforms to pitch your tent. Some of the sites sit close to the river."

Dorrie glanced about the commercial site they had secured for the next several days. "So I take it you have to carry a pack into the campsite?"

Mick nodded. "The trail's real easy, though. Perfectly level. It takes about two hours to hike, I'd say."

Dorrie sighed longingly as she plopped down on the seat next to him. "Wow, that sounds absolutely divine. Unfortunately my sister is not the roughing-it type. In fact, even this type of camping is a bit too primitive for her tastes. Gail prefers a hotel complete with an indoor pool."

Mick laughed heartily, which sparked a smile on Dorrie's face. "There's only a few women I know of who'd lug all their stuff in packs strapped to their backs just to camp in a pretty spot. I can tell you, the effort's worth it." His hand waved at their campsite. "This is fine for an overnight stay. Once you backpack in the woods, though, it's like stepping out of civilization into the wilds. You carry in everything you need and rely on no modern conveniences. There's nothing but you and nature."

"And God," Dorrie added softly, but loud enough for Mick to hear. He gave her a disconcerting look, then glanced away, pretending to study a crack running along one wooden plank that formed the picnic table.

The silence was broken by the arrival of Gail, who squealed when she saw Mick, then raced toward him and placed herself strategically in his arms. "Oh, Mick, what a nice surprise!"

"You gave me more than adequate directions, Gail," he told her, wrapping an arm around her, his eyes resting on her face.

Dorrie noticed with dismay how the two enjoyed their close proximity. Embarrassed by their actions, Dorrie busied herself with spooning out the hot oatmeal into silver bowls.

"I'm the navigator for all our trips," Gail told Mick proudly, reaching out two fingernails to flick a bit of dirt off his face. "I read the maps and plot our destinations. Dorrie has no sense of direction."

And you have no sense of propriety, flinging yourself into some stranger's arms, Dorrie fumed, but did not verbalize her thought. Instead she kept her gaze averted while setting out the bowls. "Breakfast is on. Enjoy." She then retreated toward the tent to fish out her toiletry bag.

"Aren't you going to eat anything, Dorrie?" Gail asked, a silent hope glimmering in her eyes that read *It's all right by me if you don't, then I'll have Mick all to myself!*

Dorrie shook her head. "I'm not real hungry this morning. Guess I'll hit the rest room before the crowds arrive. See you later." Dorrie strode away as fast as her legs would carry her, away from the sight of Gail and Mick sharing oatmeal at the picnic table. *Are you really all that concerned about Gail's welfare, Dorrie?* she asked herself. *Or is there a bit of jealousy hidden away inside you, like Gail says?*

Dorrie thrust the questions aside as she banged open the screen door and stepped inside the rest room. The chilly air brought forth goosebumps on her skin. She stood before the sinks, gazing once more at her reflection in the mirror and her boyish hairstyle, as her mother called it. She wondered if Mick might be turned off by her appearance, only to be attracted by the femininity of Gail, with her flouncy set of curls and makeup plastered on her face. Perhaps he did not like the idea of a female jock who loved rigorous outdoor activities.

Dorrie stared again, then unzipped her case and sorted through the junk inside until she found some lipstick. *I'm as bad as Gail*, she scolded herself, *decorating myself just so some man might notice me here in the outdoors*. She traced the color on her lips, observed the effect for a moment, then shook her head and retrieved a tissue to wipe the lipstick away. "I'm just fooling myself," Dorrie mumbled. "I should let Mick take care of Gail and I'll go hike a trail or something."

She withdrew her toothbrush and paste and vigorously scrubbed her teeth. *I can't stomach the idea of the two of them together, snuggling under my nose for the rest of this trip!* Dorrie zipped up the case and sighed. Never before had one of Gail's boyfriends upset her this much. Perhaps deep down inside she did have a longing that a godly man might one day notice her, accept her for who she was, fall in love, and ask her to marry him. While she prided herself on her single-minded devotion to the Lord, the attention shared between Gail and Mick somehow rubbed her in the wrong way. Perhaps this situation was simply a testing of her heart.

Dorrie retraced her steps to the campsite only to find Mick and Gail snuggling in each other's arms as Gail giggled over something Mick whispered in her ear. Dorrie managed to duck behind a tree before her entrance was detected. Angry tears now smarted her eyes, which she deftly wiped away. *Why God? Why do I have to go through this here, of all places? All I wanted was a quiet familylike vacation in the midst of these beautiful mountains and now I have to put up with this.* Dorrie stood silent, praying to God with all her might for a peace to prevail in the midst of these circumstances. She felt her tense muscles relax and a soothing calm replace the irritation. "Thank you, God," she whispered to her ever-present Companion and Friend, finding the strength she needed at the exact time.

Mick seemed embarrassed by Dorrie's arrival to the campsite. He leapt instantly to his feet and out of Gail's reach, swiping back his blond hair with firm strokes of his hand. Gail only glowed and offered a triumphant smile directed toward her older sister. "We saved you some breakfast," she said, showing Dorrie the pot, which now housed a lump of solid mass faintly resembling the oatmeal.

"Yeah, thanks for breakfast, it was good," Mick said, side-stepping away. "Well, I have to get back to my own campsite. Need to get packed up and all."

"You're leaving us?" Dorrie asked, hoping he would leave her and Gail alone so they might continue on with their vacation undisturbed.

Gail reached out and grasped his massive hand in hers. "Mick's offered to be our tour guide around North Conway, Dorrie, before he starts on his backpacking trip. He knows all about the town, so we don't have to worry about getting lost. Isn't that sweet of him?"

Dorrie swallowed a hard lump in her throat, then pivoted on her heel and tossed her toiletry bag into the tent.

The irritation concealed behind the gesture led Mick to comment, "You don't seem too happy about the plan, Dorrie."

"Well, this trip is supposed to be for Gail and myself," Dorrie told him flatly.

"Oh, c'mon, Dorrie," Gail said in a condescending tone of voice, "we've put up with each other for two days now. I think it's a good idea to have Mick come along instead of trying to figure out where to go and what to do once we reach town."

"There's no point in me chaperoning the two of you," Dorrie said icily. "You know the saying—two's company, three's a crowd. If you don't mind, I think I'll check out that trail to the waterfall you mentioned, Mick. Why don't you drop me off at the trailhead on the way to North Conway, then pick me up on the way back."

Mick stared at Dorrie. A look of concern flashed across his tanned features. "I don't think it's wise for you to hike alone."

"Oh, Dorrie takes care of herself," Gail informed him. "She does this all the time. . .hiking in the woods for hours. You should see her in the Catskill Mountains in New York when we stay at my aunt's summer home. She hikes everywhere and wears her Walkman, listening to all that religious music of hers. Really, if she wants to do it, let her go."

"I'll be fine," Dorrie assured him, adding silently, *Please, I need to be alone right now. . .to enjoy my stay in the White Mountains. . .and not some shopping trip with a pair of love-birds.*

"Okay, if that's what you want." Mick continued to stare at Dorrie thoughtfully as though he wanted to say more, but did not. Instead, he stuffed his hands in the pockets of his shorts with a look of disappointment overshadowing him. The reaction sent confusion and wonderment soaring through both sisters as they watched him saunter away.

❧

With all the concern inherent in an overprotective father, Mick

supplied Dorrie with an endless list of dos and don'ts as they
sat in the parking lot called Lincoln Woods, where she would
begin the hike to Franconia Falls. He gave her his topographical map of the area, pointing out the trail in detail and showing her the natural rock slide into the river. "But you need to
be careful," Mick warned. "Those rocks can be dangerous
and slippery." He sized up Dorrie's capabilities. "You sure
you can do this by yourself?"

Without waiting for Dorrie's response, Gail interjected, "Of
course she can. Dorrie's twenty-five years old and quite capable. I tell you she's used to this kind of stuff and really loves
it, don't you, Dorrie?"

"I can handle this just fine," Dorrie reassured him. "These
ole legs of mine have put on about a hundred miles and
haven't worn out yet."

"Do you have a first aid kit?" Mick asked.

"Just a small one, you know, with Band-Aids in it, that type
of thing."

Mick twisted his face and reached over into his daypack,
rummaging for a kit, which he handed to her. "You should have
a more complete one than that. Here, take mine. It has everything you need—including an ace wrap, iodine, needles. . . ."

Dorrie laughed. "I'm not contemplating major surgery on
the trail!" She waved the kit away. "I'll be fine. I've been on
dozens of trails, and by the grace of God, I've never injured
myself."

Mick poked the kit once more at her, but Dorrie pushed it
back into his chest. "Keep it. Who knows, you might need it
yourself with all that walking around in the outlet stores.
There's bound to be tons of clothing racks. You might trip
and fall over one."

Mick flushed red under the sting of her saucy remarks. He
surrendered to her pride and tossed the first aid kit back into
his pack. "Okay, you win. I guess that's everything. We'll

meet you back here around five. That should give you plenty of time for the hike and some recreation."

Dorrie hoisted up her daypack and adjusted the straps around her shoulders. "Well, you two have a good time now."

Gail gave her sister an affectionate hug, whispering, "Thanks for giving us the day to ourselves, Dorrie. You're a terrific sis."

"Sure," Dorrie said, avoiding the look in her sister's eye. "Anytime."

Mick sat quietly in the driver's seat, rapping his fingers on the steering wheel, lost in thought. He glanced up when Dorrie threw a final wave good-bye, then grabbed hold of the steering wheel as Gail jumped into the passenger seat next to him. No one noticed the strange moodiness that suddenly overcame him.

Once Dorrie's feet hit the trail, a sense of well-being soared through her. The day was beautiful, with clear blue skies and a refreshing breeze that caressed her face with soft, sweeping strokes. The daypack bounced up and down on her back as she took long strides with her legs, propelling her forward to Franconia Falls. The level trail appeared like an endless road in the midst of the great forest. As sunlight streamed through the woods, Dorrie noted the various shades of green found in the forest—from avocado, to a sea green, to a rich, deep moss. Birds serenaded the walk from branches overhanging the trail. Occasional passersby would offer a quick hello, with some asking Dorrie how far it was back to the trailhead. In return she inquired of the distance left to the falls. Dorrie relished the comradery she discovered when sharing the trail with fellow hikers. She sensed a unique relationship with those that lived and breathed the great outdoors.

Dorrie observed this with Mick when he offered her his medical kit and graciously provided her his topographical map. As he sat next to her in the car, explaining the route, Dorrie could detect in his voice an excitement for the woods and a distinct yearning to hike the trails he loved. She wondered if he would rather be hiking with her to Franconia Falls than browsing the outlet stores with her giddy sister. "If that were true, well, I wouldn't be doing this journey alone," Dorrie reminded herself, stepping around a rock lying in the middle of the path.

She thought back to her conversation with Mick by the Old Man of the Mountain, wondering what calamity spawned his falling out with God. Hanging around a person like Gail, who did not share a Christian viewpoint, would not restore Mick into a right relationship with God. Dorrie sighed, her steps lengthening along the natural walkway. She should reach out to him, discover the pain of the past, and help bring healing to his heart. Maybe it was possible to turn his life around so it would once again burn with a renewed commitment to the purposes of God.

After several miles of hiking, Dorrie squinted her eyes to see the dark image of a wooden cabin in the distance, signaling the caretaker hut for the Franconia Brook Campsite. She passed several wooden platforms where tents were pitched, surrounded by an assortment of gear. Huge metal boxes near the campsites served as caches for food supplies to keep curious bears from raiding camp supplies. Dorrie stopped to admire one campsite with a baby blue tent. Sleeping bags airdried over a stout clothesline hung between two trees. A small cooking stove sat next to a fire pit where a huge pile of wood had been gathered, presumably for a roaring fire that evening. The whole scene proved pleasing to Dorrie and one she would love to experience some day.

Reluctantly she plodded forward until she heard the roar of the water and found the raging river and rocks speckled with people of all ages. Some scampered barefoot on the rocks while others sunbathed or waded in the cool waters. Dorrie hiked along the riverbank until she came to a point where the rocks split wide open to form a perfect chute directly into a deep pool of water below. Excitement bubbled up within her as she watched several young kids glide down the natural rock slide with shrieks of laughter, their arms waving in the air as they splashed into the waters below. Eager to be a part, Dorrie stripped off her clothes, revealing a modest one-piece swimsuit, and came to the riverbank.

"Is the water cold?" she asked one shivering youngster as he grabbed a beach towel off a nearby rock and wrapped it around his wet form.

"Naw, it's fun!" he assured her.

"Where do you go in at?"

"Right there." He pointed to a place in the rock just before it formed a steep slide under the rapid flow of the river. "You get in there and slide on down. It's a blast!"

Dorrie smiled at the boy, then joined a line of people waiting their turn at the slide. She splashed some of the chilly water along her arms and across the front of her suit, wincing as the cold shocked her flesh and sent goosebumps rising to the surface. The roar of the water as it dashed over the rocks filled her ears, reminding her of the ocean waves that crashed along the sandy beaches of Long Island.

At the beaches, the crowds were thick like fleas, the sand checkered with various shades of red, yellow, green, and blue from towels strewn across the sand. Umbrellas would poke out of the sand like stunted trees to provide shade, while children and adults alike shouted as they romped in the waters. Dorrie sighed, thankful to be here in the mountains, away from the hordes of people sharing the ocean and the faint outline of the Manhattan skyline visible in the distance. Here there was only the roar of a mountain stream, clear blue skies unmarred by smog, and the refreshing air scented by balsam.

All of a sudden, it was Dorrie's turn at the rock slide. She sat down gingerly in the icy water, shivering a bit, then pushed off. Down, down, down she went, careening into the cold water below. "Woowee!" Dorrie cried in utter delight, shaking the water from her face while pushing back strings of hair dripping water in her eyes. She scrambled up the embankment, eager to try it again. After six or so turns plunging into the crystal-clear pool, Dorrie took a break by the riverbank. She toweled off her hair, then nourished herself with a granola bar and some water from her plastic water bottle.

"I wonder how hiker Mick and Miss Gail are enjoying the outlets," Dorrie mused, biting into the bar while watching the children scamper on the rocks. "It certainly can't be as much fun as this." With a bit of nourishment in her stomach, Dorrie found a warm place on the rocks, spread out her towel and sunbathed for a time, allowing the sun's rays to dry her damp skin and suit. "This is wonderful," she breathed, closing her eyes. "If heaven is even half as nice as this place, it will be marvelous!"

After some time in the sun, Dorrie felt the rock slide beckoning her once more before she had to hike back to rendezvous with the shopping duo by five o'clock. Glancing at her watch in the pocket of her daypack, Dorrie decided she had time left for a few quick trips down the slide before changing back into her hiking attire. The crowds had dissipated by then, leaving Dorrie alone as she ambled up to the starting point. Down she went, her arms flying over her head, and with a splash, hit the pool. She rose quickly to the surface, her eyes scanning the slide above her. "Should I go one more time?" she debated. "Oh, why not? One more time, then I'll head back to meet the lovebirds. Tweet, tweet!" Dorrie giggled.

Slowly she climbed up to the top of the rocky formation once more, conscious of the fatigue that gripped her legs. With effort, Dorrie nestled in the slit between the rocks and pushed off. As she slid down the rocks, a terrible cramp suddenly seized one leg muscle in a painful hold. With a cry, Dorrie lurched uncontrollably into the water, her ankle twisting in several rocks found in the pool below.

Fighting to regain control, Dorrie paddled with her arms while trying to ignore the gnawing sensation of pain rising in her ankle. She managed to reach the shore and struggled onto a rock, where she examined the damage to the injured extremity.

"Great," Dorrie groaned. "I twisted up my leg real good." She managed to scoot herself to the bank where her daypack lay and sat nursing the wounded leg. "Oh, Lord, now what do I do?" Dorrie moaned in despair, glancing around the deserted riverbank. "I can't even walk! How am I ever going to get myself back down the trail like this?"

four

The sun began to dip below the trees, with shadows of the approaching night resting across the landscape. After changing out of her damp swimsuit behind a rock, Dorrie limped several yards away from the river's edge to an open area of the woods, where she now leaned up against a stately old tree for support. Her red bandanna, drenched in the cold water from the river, lay swathed around her swollen ankle, but this did little to ease the pain or remedy her predicament.

Dorrie realized the impossibility of hiking without adequate support on her injured ankle. For a time she sat still, her arms crossed before her chest, angry words poised on her lips that she refused to mutter aloud. Instead her mind argued with the question *Why?* Why did she take that last leap into the water knowing her fatigue from the day's activities? Why did God allow this to happen just when she was having such a glorious time in His creation? She thought of the ace wrap nestled in Mick's first aid kit as her ankle throbbed with pain. Remembering his offer to lend her the kit, Dorrie realized that her own stubbornness had prevented her from accepting the one item that might have assisted her in the walk back. "It's all my fault," she spoke aloud, lending a sigh of exasperation.

Dorrie fumbled with the makeshift bandage around her ankle, trying to tie it more firmly. She thought of hobbling over to one of the campsites and asking for assistance, but the mere thought of stumbling into some stranger's camp left her feeling uncomfortable. "Well, Dorrie, oh girl, you wanted a camp-out in the woods, and it looks like you might get your wish."

Dorrie sifted through the contents inside her pack, sizing

up the food that remained—one granola bar and a box of raisins. A half-filled bottle of potable water sat next to her. Dorrie sighed. "I suppose this'll have to do for dinner. I don't have many options right now." She consumed the sparse meal, then rested against the rough bark of the tree, watching the sun slowly disappear behind a grove of trees. The blue sky melted into colors of orange and red with the coming twilight. Crickets began to serenade her with their nightly choruses. Dorrie shivered with her arms cradled around her legs, wondering how she would keep warm in the cool mountains without a blanket. Inside her pack lay a wadded sweatshirt, which she shrugged on. Her bare legs cramped with the cold, sending ripples of pain shooting down into her injured ankle. "This is not what I had planned, God," Dorrie grumbled in frustration. "How am I supposed to make it through the night like this?"

In a firm determination to try and resume the hike, Dorrie gathered up her belongings and struggled to her feet. A terrible pain gripped her ankle as she fought to take a few meager steps before resigning herself to the reality of her injury. Once more she occupied a space on the ground. "Gail will probably be worried by now," Dorrie decided, readjusting the damp bandanna around her ankle. "Then again, maybe she's thanking God that I gave her more time to spend with Mister Wonderful."

A rustling in the woods disturbed Dorrie's contemplations. Her eyes scanned the glade of thick trees that now turned into dark, ominous statues before her. A squirrel dashed from a web of tangled brush, scampered along the ground, then scooted up the nearest tree waving his bushy tail. "Wish I could run like you," Dorrie called out wistfully to the squirrel. Once more a wave of cold air swept over her. "I should build some type of fire," she reasoned out loud, enjoying the companionship of her voice, "but I can't begin to gather up the wood for it, so what's the use?"

Dorrie soon drifted off into an uneasy sleep, twitching every so often with cold as she dreamt of Mick dangling an ace wrap in front of her face. She heard voices calling her name in the dream. Dorrie stirred, then bolted upright, wincing at the pain in her ankle. Again she heard the faint voice of someone calling her name.

"Dorrie? Dorrie?"

"Here!" she cried. "Here I am!"

"Keep calling to me," the voice directed.

Dorrie yelled out, "Here, right over here," until branches were batted away and a tall form approached her from the woods. The dark figure was Mick, wearing a daypack and carrying a flashlight. Wrinkles of concern lay etched in deep crevices across his darkened face. Immediately he came to her side, inquiring about her condition in an anxious voice.

"I'm okay, really," Dorrie mumbled, flushing with embarrassment over the idea of her injury requiring Mick to come rescue her like a superhero.

His strong, gentle hands worked across the swollen flesh of her ankle, assessing the extent of her injury. "Might be broken," Mick gravely noted, turning to locate some downed tree limbs. "I'm going to make you a splint for that ankle."

Dorrie shivered again as a brisk breeze blew. Noticing her cold, Mick threw open his pack and pulled out a pair of his sweats for her to put on. "W. . .where's Gail?" Dorrie stammered as she donned the warm fleece over her chilled extremities.

"Well, when you didn't show up at five and then at six, I had a feeling something was wrong. I drove Gail across the highway to the campground there and set up my tent. She didn't want me to leave her alone, but I told her she'd be fine in the tent." Mick worked efficiently, tearing up one of his bandannas into strips to tie around the makeshift splint that now cradled her ankle. He then fastened the whole contraption snugly into place with an ace wrap.

"Where did you learn to do all that?" Dorrie noted in admiration as she watched him work.

"Boy Scouts."

"Boy Scouts?" She smiled at the mere thought of the man as a scout in his younger days, wearing a kerchief around his neck and quoting the Boy Scout honor code with raised fingers.

"We had to learn various first aid techniques to earn one of the badges," he explained. With the task completed, Mick sat back on his heels. "How'd you do this to yourself, anyway?"

"I wasn't very smart. I wanted one more slide down the rocks into the water, even though I knew I was tired out. The rock slide's a great place, just like you said it would be."

He nodded his head. "So you injured yourself on the last trip down?"

"Yup, last trip, always the very last one you plan on making, you know." Conscious of eyes perusing her, Dorrie kept her gaze averted, focusing her attention on her ankle and the sticks cradling it, secured by the ace wrap from his first aid kit.

"That's always the way it is," Mick confirmed, rising to his feet. His tall, commanding presence proved comforting in the dark surroundings. His heavy footsteps crushed the leaves scattered across the forest floor as his hands brushed through the downed vegetation, looking for an implement to assist with walking. In a short time he returned with a forked stick. "Okay, let's see if you can walk using this stick as a crutch. If not, I'll run back to the caretaker cabin and ask the guy to radio out for help."

Dorrie blushed at the embarrassment of having to be carried down the trail on a stretcher. With effort and the help of Mick's strong forearm, she hoisted herself to a standing position. She gritted her teeth and said, "It's gonna be slow I'm afraid."

Mick frowned as she hobbled alongside him to the trail, which appeared dark and uninviting with the approach of night. "I don't think this is going to work," he told her. "Let me try to get you back to the caretaker's cabin, where I can get you some help."

"Mick, I'll absolutely die if someone has to carry me out on a stretcher," Dorrie pleaded. "I'll get myself down this trail and back to the parking area if it's the last thing I do."

Mick grunted in reservation but allowed her to lean heavily on him, using him for support. "This would be fine and dandy if we only had half a mile to go," he grumbled, struggling to maintain his own stability while balancing her at the same time, "but it's over two miles to the parking area. There's absolutely no way you can make it like this."

"Then I will pray, and if you don't mind, maybe you can say a prayer for me, too." She began her prayer in earnest, the words jarring from her lips as she fought to keep herself balanced on the uneven path. "Lord, please give me the strength I need to make this walk. Help the swelling go down so I might walk better. Give Mick the strength to assist me. Thank you for watching over us and protecting us in everything we do. In Jesus name, Amen."

After a time, Mick said, "You're walking a little better now."

"The power of prayer," Dorrie breathed, a grin filling her face. Using the stick for leverage, Dorrie released her hold on Mick and began limping along on her own.

Mick watched her progression in some surprise. After a time they passed several boulders nestled alongside the trail and decided on a brief rest stop. "Guess the ankle loosened up when you began to exercise it," he noted.

Dorrie laughed. "A true scientific mind at work," she teased him. "You know it's not that. I prayed for help and God answered it."

Mick gulped down the water from his bottle before recorking it with a pound of his fist. "That may be, but more often than not, I've found God to be pretty deaf whenever I pray."

"Depends on what you pray for," Dorrie said matter-of-factly while examining her makeshift wooden splint, oblivious to his growing discontent. "He won't answer something that's not according to His perfect will."

After a few painful minutes, Mick blurted out, "Well, I asked for something that deserved to be answered. I sure never asked Him for all the persecution heaped on us, and finally the. . ." He hesitated, then bent over as if the weight of the secret he carried within proved overbearing. His fingers groped for his feet, looking to tighten the laces that had loosened on his hiking boots.

Dorrie realized Mick sat poised to reveal the reason underlining his strained relationship with God. She waited for what seemed like an eternity before prodding him with a question. "What kind of persecution, Mick?"

"Never mind," he snapped, rising to his feet. He looked down on her, then offered her a hand up. "C'mon. Gail probably thinks we got lost or something."

They continued on in silence as Mick withdrew a flashlight from a side pouch to his daypack and turned it on. The trail glowed before them. An owl hooted in the woods nearby. Evening crickets continued in their singsongs. For a time only the breathing from the exercise was shared between the two until Mick suddenly said, "Sorry I snapped at you back there."

"It's okay." Dorrie then inhaled a deep breath before remarking, "Sounds like you went through a rough time."

"Yeah, I did." Mick flashed the beam of light across the portion of trail Dorrie now hobbled on. "Like I said, it made me even question God's existence. . .why He lets people go through the things they go through in life." He paused, then added, "I thought He took care of His children but it seems like He makes them go through hell on earth first as a prerequisite for heaven or something."

"Even Jesus said we would be persecuted, Mick," Dorrie reminded him. "As they persecuted Him so they will persecute us."

"Yeah, right." His boots pounded the ground in agitation. "I didn't mind the name calling and everything, but when the gang members hurt our family, it became impossible to trust in God anymore. It's like He decided to abandon us."

Tingles shot through Dorrie, sending the hairs on the back of her neck standing straight up. Her curiosity nearly drove her to the breaking point.

"Dad was a good, decent, honorable man," Mick went on, his voice hardening as he continued to reveal bits and pieces of the mystery surrounding his life, "but now he sits in a chair in some nursing home all day long and doesn't even recognize his own family." His breathing became raucous as he flared, "What kind of merciful God would send one of His preachers into a life like that, Dorrie?"

Dorrie gulped. Her hand gripped the stick tightly as she plodded along, dragging her injured extremity behind her. "I. . .I can't answer that, Mick. Was your Dad a preacher or something?"

"Yeah, Dad loved to preach. His calling was street evangelism. He had a heart for the gangs of inner Boston, but the gang sure rewarded him. They took everything away from him when the leader fired that bullet into his brain." His feet now stomped the ground in anger and hurt. "Dad lay in a coma for over a year and a half. When he came out of it, he didn't know anything or anyone. It's like he reverted back to infancy or something." Suddenly Mick stopped, his fists clenched as he stood straight and immobile, his eyes focused straight ahead. "I hate God for allowing the gang to do that to my father. God put him in that state. Dad gave his life to serve God and then God repays him with a bullet in the brain and a life as a vegetable in a chair." His face now turned to acknowledge Dorrie. "So don't tell me anymore about a loving God or praying to God for help or even believing in a God. As far as I'm concerned, there is no God."

Dorrie felt her heart would break under these statements. Silently she murmured prayers for Mick, but knew nothing could reach a heart hardened in cement from the pain of his past. All she could do was show mercy as she was sure God wanted to show him—the mercy of One who understood even if Mick was opposed to Him. Dorrie cast the stick away and approached him, reaching out with as much compassion as she could muster. "I'm so sorry, Mick," she choked, surprised by the tears welling up in her eyes. "What a terrible thing to have to go through."

Mick accepted Dorrie's embrace, holding her as his muscles heaved under the weight of the burdens he bore. Finally he whispered, "I. . .I've never confided any of this to a stranger before. I don't know why I told you, but it's like I had to tell someone right now. With you being injured and all tonight, it seemed the right place and the right time."

Dorrie disengaged herself from his arms and hobbled back to retrieve her stick. Instead of bitterness for her sprained ankle, her heart found a reason to be thankful. Through the injury, God had opened a door of communication with this troubled man that might have not otherwise existed. "I'm glad you told me, Mick. I have to admit, ever since you mentioned a problem in your past back at the Old Man, I was curious to know what happened. I knew you went through some kind of heartache in your life, but of course, I didn't know what."

Mick stared at her thoughtfully. "You seem like someone I can open up to, Dorrie. It's hard to believe you and Gail are sisters. . .you're both so different. Gail is refreshing because she is like a little girl who loves to have fun with life. You, though, you're very serious, you look at things as they are. . ."

"Some have told me I'm a black and white person," Dorrie confessed. "I see black and white, nothing else."

Mick nodded in agreement. "That's right, you do. You aren't after the fluff or the wide picture. You're a person who looks right at reality without being sidetracked into other things." He sighed, his flashlight acknowledging a painted blaze on a tree nearby. "Guess we ought to get going."

They continued on down the trail, discussing likes and dislikes. Dorrie was amazed to discover they shared many interests, not only for the great outdoors, but in traveling the United States in search of an exciting adventure, or in the area of scientific studies. Mick commented, "Don't mention this to Gail, but I could never settle down with someone who doesn't like to backpack in the outdoors or who doesn't appreciate biology. My hikes and my students are the most important areas in my life right now. They mean everything to me."

After he had spoken these words, Dorrie sensed a strange tingle sweep over her and shoot through each extremity. She realized then how much she loved to backpack and recalled her keen interest in hearing of Mick's escapades teaching biology. In fact, she fulfilled many of his ideas surrounding a perfect companion. Instead of pondering the significance of the statement, Dorrie switched tactics to ease the anxiety mounting within her. "Well, if Gail were to find out how much you love hiking, she'd probably put on her hiking boots and tramp the trails. You know she already thinks you're out of this world."

Mick smirked. "I had a feeling," he agreed, "but I'm not so sure it's meant to be." He then mentioned the incident at the campsite when Dorrie discovered them sharing an embrace. "Sorry you had to put up with all that at the campsite this morning. It was rude and unfair to you." After thinking for a few moments, he added, "Gail can be pretty wild at times. I think she has some idea about us having a relationship, but I don't think that's such a wise idea."

Dorrie could not help but agree, thankful Mick had seen the light where Gail was concerned. "Mick, I think the best thing for all of us is to have you drive us back to our campsite and leave us there to continue on with our vacation and you with yours. In that way no one will feel pressured or unhappy and everyone can have a good time." The moment Dorrie suggested this, she regretted the words. The mere thought of Mick leaving, never to be seen again, saddened her in a strange sort of way.

"I'd rather see how you're feeling before I make my great escape."

"Well, don't ruin your vacation on account of my stupidity, Mick. You should go and enjoy yourself in the White Mountains while you have the time."

There was silence for a few moments before his voice acknowledged, much to Dorrie's astonishment, "I am enjoying myself very much."

ъ

Dorrie and Mick arrived at the dark campsite to find Gail asleep on top of his sleeping bag inside the tent. Mick lit his propane lantern, then fished out freeze-dried food for them to eat. Finding herself famished after the long, eventful day, Dorrie gratefully accepted the jerky, apricots, crackers, and other food. Sitting opposite Mick at the picnic table with the food spread out before her, Dorrie contemplated how she would pray for the food and his reaction to the gesture.

In answer to her unspoken dilemma, Mick motioned to her with a stick of jerky. "Go ahead and pray for your food if you want, Dorrie. I'm not going to stop you from having your own beliefs."

Dorrie shrugged, bent her head, and offered a prayer. Then in an afterthought, she added, "And help Mick know how much you care Lord, and how much you love him and his family for the sacrifices they have made. Amen." Dorrie opened her eyes to find Mick staring hard at her, his eyes burning as they reflected the light of the lantern. Even his blond hair seemed to radiate with the flames of anger roaring within him.

"Don't pray for me anymore."

"Somebody has to, Mick. . ." Dorrie began until his hand came up, silencing her.

"No, nobody has to. I've had many people pray over me. It has already been said time and time again. I know you're just trying to be helpful, but I think it's best if you leave God out of my life."

Dorrie fumbled for the jerky sitting before her. With her vision marred by the tears forming in her eyes, the food wavered like ripples on the water. A large lump in the pit of her stomach silenced the hunger pains. She forced herself to pick up the jerky and chew it while focusing her attention once more on the lantern and the moths attracted to the flame. *Not only does Gail need You, God, but Mick does, too. He needs to draw near to You, the light of life, before he falls any deeper into this pit of bitterness.*

five

Mick elected to spend the night in his car while Dorrie made herself comfortable on a few blankets spread inside the tent next to the snoring form of her sister. Before retiring for the night, Dorrie ventured shyly to the picnic table where Mick sat absorbed in a trail guide and map. When he turned to acknowledge her, the light from the lantern cast a sheen of white over her.

"I just wanted to thank you for coming out after me tonight."

He smiled. "No problem. Glad you're feeling better. You think you might want to go to a hospital in the morning and get an x-ray of your ankle?"

Dorrie flexed her ankle. "It really is feeling better. I think I just sprained it. Anyway, I was wondering if you had any aspirin, just to avoid any flare-up of pain during the night."

Mick nodded and reached for his daypack lying on the ground, rummaging for his first aid kit. Watching his activity, Dorrie remarked, "Yeah, I was full of pride, telling you to keep that kit for yourself when I sure needed the ace wrap stored inside. It's like you had a premonition something would go wrong. . .like you knew I would need it."

"Yeah, what's the old saying, Dorrie? Pride comes before the fall?" Mick chuckled at first, then grew despondent as the words of Scripture sunk deep into him. He thumped his chest as if to ward off the biting insect of conviction nipping his soul, then gave her two tablets and the water bottle. "Have a good night's sleep."

"Thanks, you too."

Dorrie returned to the tent, unaware of Mick's eyes probing her every move, his thoughts reverberating with her simple but powerful confession. Now as he returned his attention to the map before him, he considered her offers of help on the trail to bind the wounds of his past. *Dorrie offered me a bandage, too,* he realized, *but how can some stranger repair a heart that has been torn to shreds?* Once more the word "pride" echoed in his thoughts. Mick shook his head. The map before him wavered as visions of his father's attack in a cold, dark alley of Boston now haunted him. He could still hear the sound of the pistol firing behind his father's unsuspecting back and the terrible thud as Dad collapsed onto the hard pavement. Crimson blood dribbled from the head wound. A shiver swept over Mick as he squeezed his eyes shut, trying to blot out the painful memories that tumbled like a car careening off a cliff. Instead, he pictured himself kneeling next to his father's side, trying in vain to arouse him even as one of the gang members threatened him with the same smoking weapon.

"That'll teach him to keep his mouth shut about Jesus," the leader of the gang snarled at Mick.

The wail of a police siren sent the gang members scurrying for cover as Mick hovered over his father's unconscious form, calling his name. An ambulance was summoned, and before Mick realized it, rescue people clad in uniforms whisked his father away to the hospital. Mick could still taste the saltiness of his tears running into his mouth as he stumbled along the street, then drifted down a staircase to the subway station. He wondered how his mother would react to the news that her husband had just been gunned down in an obscure alley of Boston's dark streets.

For years Mom warned Dad to stay away from the gangs for fear he might become a target of their vengeance. The news of laymen and ministers murdered in South America and other parts of the world left her quaking in great fear.

Often Mick would hear her murmur prayers well into the wee hours of the morning. . .words that now seemed to have fallen on deaf ears.

When Mick arrived home in Cambridge—a suburb of Boston and home to the prestigious Harvard University—he found his mother on the phone. She cried as a stranger's voice relayed the sad news of her husband's critical state after suffering a gunshot wound to the head.

Throwing the phone into the cradle on the wall, she grabbed her purse and, along with Mick, rushed to the hospital in the center of the great city of Boston. They arrived to find his father in emergency surgery to stop the bleeding in his skull. For hours and hours they waited, huddled together, drawing strength from one another while the delicate procedure was performed.

When the neurosurgeon finally appeared in a doctor's white coat covering the green garb of the operating room, he told the family the news they feared most—Dad suffered untold amount of damage to the brain. He now lived on life support. They were uncertain he would ever regain consciousness. Mom cried uncontrollably, leaning on Mick for support, until she asked him to contact his older sister, who lived with her family out in California.

Mick telephoned Pamela, who flew in the very next day. In her usual bossy manner, Pam took control of the situation immediately by arranging a conference with the physicians responsible for Dad's care so the family might reason out the situation. On the homefront, Pam fixed the meals, telephoned the neighbors and relatives with news of the dreadful occurrence, handled the influx of newspaper and television re-porters, and maintained order. Mick only found himself paralyzed during the awful time, trapped by the knowledge of this terrible loss and the endless question of why? Why, when Dad gave everything to the druggies and winos and mixed-up kids on the street did God forsake him in his hour of need? Why did God allow such a tragedy to enfold their tiny family unit?

Dad was eventually weaned from the respirator but remained in his coma. Mom visited every day, talking to him, reading from the Bible, sharing the family news, even though his eyes remained closed and he never acknowledged a word she spoke. Mick came less and less frequently to the acute care center where they had placed him. Instead he delved into his studies, sent out resumes, and secured a teaching position at one of the area middle schools. During the time he remained at home, he used the money he earned to help pay the bills. Little by little he ceased reading the Bible, praying, or attending church. He did not even acknowledge the church support that went out to the family during the crisis. Several in the church raised funds through bake sales and special collections to help offset the massive medical bills mounting from Dad's care. Others brought over food once a week or came to cheer up his mother, who relished the visits. Yet this outpouring of love from the church family did little to ease the torture inflicting Mick.

Pam offered to move back from California to help manage everything, but Mom refused, encouraging her to continue on with her own life. Mick was secretly glad when Pam left for the West Coast, for she tended to lord it over him as his big sister. Mick held the impression that Pam never considered him an adult but the kid brother who remained interested in playing toy soldiers or hitting a baseball. Even during the height of Dad's illness, she became authoritative, ordering him to do this or that. Mick sighed in relief when he watched her plane take off from Logan International Airport, whispering under his breath so his mother could not hear, "Good-bye, so long, and good riddance."

One day, eighteen months after the initial injury, an exciting thing happened. Mick remembered escorting his mother to his car after a visit with Dad when a nurse came flying out of the entrance to the care unit, waving her arms frantically. "He's waking up, Mrs. Walters! Quick!"

Mick and his mother dashed back inside the facility to see Dad groaning and stirring in his sleep. Mom called out to him in an anxious voice. When his eyes opened, he only stared at her with a blank expression, mumbling some sort of gibberish they did not understand.

"It takes time," the nurse assured them. "Why, he's been asleep for eighteen months. Let's just give him time and see what he does."

However, time only served to show Mick and his mother the true extent of the damage suffered by the bullet that pierced the street preacher's brain. Dad would blubber and bawl, croak out one-word phrases, and sometimes throw temper tantrums by dashing his food to the floor. He was incontinent, requiring adult-size pads to keep him dry. The more Mick witnessed this altered mental state, the more bitter he became. Unable to bear it anymore, Mick moved out of the house, rented his own apartment, and refused to visit his father.

"Mick, really, I have seen changes in your father," his mother would say, begging him to visit his father. "Why, I know he looks at me and answers me when I speak. Please, he needs to see you. He needs you so bad."

"That person isn't my father," Mick told her in a stiff voice, hatred burning in his eyes. "That's a stranger, some. . . some baby with an adult face. He doesn't even know who I am! Sorry, Mom, but I can't take it. I won't accept it. As far as I'm concerned, Dad might as well be dead."

Soon afterwards, Mom sold the home that had been the family's for as long as Mick could remember and purchased a small condo near the long-term care facility, where she could be close to Dad. Mick occasionally visited to share dinner with her, but refused to visit his father. Whenever Mom would pray or bring out her Bible, he would scorn her beliefs and inform her that no loving God would have done this to his father, especially when he devoted his whole life to serving Him and the kingdom. Mom cried in response to his accusations, sending waves of guilt washing over Mick. She sent her pastor to Mick's apartment in an effort to reach her embittered son, but Mick would only shout, curse, and threaten the man until the pastor was obliged to leave him alone. "His heart is like stone," the pastor informed his mother. "Only God Himself can reach the young man in a way we have yet to see ourselves. Keep him in prayer."

Now as Mick's eyes surveyed the tent and the occupants within, he wondered if Dorrie was indeed the answer to the ceaseless prayers offered on his behalf. In a way, Mick prided himself on being the prodigal son—the one who refused to accept his father's condition as the will of God. Mick scowled at the mere thought of Dorrie's Christian beliefs, vowing never to allow her the opportunity to break through the protective barriers encasing his heart in marble.

After awhile, Mick turned off the propane lantern and switched on his flashlight, preparing to venture to the car, where he would spend an uncomfortable night curled up in the passenger's seat. A multitude of stars shone crystal clear in the night sky, indicative of a pleasant day the following morning. Mick wondered what the day would hold as he opened the car door and settled himself inside. Initially he had planned to begin a backpacking excursion into the vast wilderness, but circumstances forced a one-day delay in his plans. Now as he reclined in the seat with his arms crossed behind his head, he thought of the sisters occupying his tent and how each filled voids in his life he never knew existed.

❧

The next morning both women emerged from the tent

refreshed from their night's sleep, only to find their protector readying his pack for a lengthy hike. Neither spoke a word to him despite the fact each sensed a mixture of sorrow and disappointment over his decision to begin his hike. Soon Gail began pleading with Mick not to abandon her just when they were all having a good time.

Irritated by her sister's continual pestering of Mick, Dorrie drew the fretful Gail to one side and told her that it was time they went on with their vacation and left Mick to enjoy his. "He's spent enough time with us already. We're here to have our own vacations."

Gail glared at her older sister. "Yeah, that's fine for you to say, Dorrie, after spending the whole night out with *my* boyfriend!"

"He's not your boyfriend."

"Oh, he's not? And just how would you know? Don't think I didn't hear you two chatting and who knows what else, real cozylike at the picnic table last night." Gail whirled away to avoid her sister's startled expression.

"Gail Marie Shelton, all we did was talk!" Dorrie fired back. "That's it, period. Maybe next time instead of eavesdropping, you'll have the nerve to come out of hiding and find out what we're doing."

Gail gave a huff and strode off angrily toward the roar of the river that lay beyond the tent sites. Dorrie exhaled in exasperation, her breath fanning the wisps of dark brown bangs across her forehead.

All at once, Mick came to investigate the commotion. "So am I the cause of the arguing today?" he wondered.

"Gail's jealous. Why. . .I haven't a clue. She thinks we were doing something inappropriate at the picnic table last night to which I promptly set the record straight." Dorrie turned to face him. "Guess between last night's fiasco and the idea you're leaving on a hike today, this gives her enough reason to pout.

Honestly, I don't know why we decided to do this trip together. I thought it would be good for the two of us to get out into the woods and renew a friendship, but all we seem to do is get into fights." Dorrie picked up a twig from the ground and pitched it in disgust. "When we get back to the campsite, I might as well pack up the gear and head for home. There's no way I'm gonna endure any more of this." Then in an afterthought she added, "There's a hundred bucks up in smoke."

"A hundred bucks?" Mick repeated in confusion. "What costs a hundred bucks?"

"For our stay at the Lakes of the Clouds hut on Mount Washington. I wanted it to be the finale to our vacation. . . a glorious jaunt up to the highest peak of the Presidential mountain range and then a magnificent stay at the most popular hiker's hut. Now, between my ankle and our quarreling, it doesn't look like we're gonna make it."

Mick eyed her in amazement. "That's pretty wild because I have reservations at the same hut midway through my hike. What day is your reservation for?"

"Friday night."

Mick laughed. "Same as mine. Look, Dorrie, today's only Wednesday and you have several days left to rest that ankle of yours. Since you really want to do the hike, you can give Gail a little incentive to stick it out by telling her I'll be waiting for her to show up at the hut Friday night."

Dorrie's face brightened. "That's not a bad idea. Just knowing you'll be waiting at the top of the mountain might make the trip easier to swallow for the both of us." Dorrie's gaze drifted toward the river and the faint outline of her sister, skipping rocks by the shore. "Well, I'd better help you break camp and all. I hope you don't mind driving us back to our campsite."

"No problem," he assured her. "I'm going to a trailhead in that general area anyway, so it works out well with my plans."

Together they grabbed hold of the tent poles, dismantled them, then gently eased the shelter to the ground. The poles were pushed out of the sleeves of the tent and the fabric stuffed into a large nylon sack. By the time Gail arrived back, the site was spic and span, with remnants of the gear stowed away in Mick's car. As Mick and Dorrie surveyed the site for any remaining camping gear that might have been overlooked, Gail's drawn face observed all of this in growing agitation.

Dorrie waved her arm toward her younger sister. "Let's go, Gail," she called out, sliding into the passenger seat of Mick's car.

Gail stood her ground and shook her head fiercely like a strong-willed child ready to unleash a terrible tantrum.

"What's eating her?" Mick questioned Dorrie, who shrugged her shoulders. Dorrie grasped the underside of her injured extremity, eased her leg out, and stood to her feet. "C'mon now, Gail. We gotta get back to the campsite and make sure no one's ripped off our stuff." Dorrie hobbled up to Gail, who remained in her stubborn stance, her teeth gnawing on her bottom lip. "What's wrong with you?"

Gail sniffed at Dorrie's injured ankle. "I'll bet you just got yourself injured so you'd get *my* boyfriend all sympathetic," she muttered. "Now he's running off into the woods and leaving me behind, all because of you."

Dorrie's face flushed. "That's not true. Mick's been planning this hike of his all along. If anything, we're the ones who interrupted his plans." She then lowered her voice. "Look, you'll see Mick again in no time, if that's any consolation. He's planning on a stay at the same hiker hut I have reservations for at the end of the week. And he just told me he can't wait to see you again."

Gail's eyes sparkled in anticipation. "Really? What hut is this?"

"You know. . .that hut I've been telling you about since we

arrived here in the Whites, the one parked on the shoulder of Mount Washington called Lakes of the Clouds."

Gail rolled her eyes. "Oh, that one. Yeah, you told me I had to hike three steep miles to get to the thing. No way. I'll never make it."

"C'mon, not even for Mick?" Dorrie asked with a persuasive tilt to her voice. "You wouldn't want to leave him stranded on the summit now, would you?"

Gail's eyes darkened as she crossed her arms tightly before her. "What's the sense, Dorrie, seeing as you've already claimed him for yourself?"

"Look, Gail, we've got to get going. We're holding Mick up. I promise with all my heart I won't even speak to him while we're there, okay? You can have him all to yourself. I won't get in your way. I'll just be like a cloud passing through the sky."

Gail laughed scornfully. "Yeah, right. How do I know you'll keep your word?"

Dorrie sensed the indignation rising within her, but quickly suppressed it with a deep breath. "You have my word. Scouts honor or whatever. Now come on, we're making Mick late for his hike. Go ahead and sit in the front seat if you want."

Gail finally nodded and hopped brightly into the seat next to Mick, while Dorrie gingerly occupied the rear passenger seat, wedging herself beside a box containing camping equipment. The smell of propane assaulted her nostrils, mixed with the musty odor of canvas material. Mick shifted the small car into gear and rolled out of the campground and onto the Kancamagus Highway. Occasionally his blue eyes would survey Dorrie from the rearview mirror with an expression that illustrated an eagerness to converse with her rather than the chatty Gail, who clung to his arm while her tongue flip-flopped inside her mouth. Soon they were speeding their way through a beautiful area known as Franconia Notch, where steep stone mountainsides split wide open to encompass the thin stretch of highway. The crevices of rock formed unique gorges, while the mountains offered hikers the challenge of climbs that would bring them high into the alpine tundra. Spectacular views from the rock-strewn summits rewarded the climbers.

Mick veered the car off the highway and passed the little wooden hut where the two women first laid eyes on him and his pack, ready to tackle the strenuous trails existing in the region. Finally he pulled into the campsite where Dorrie's car sat parked. The campsite was none the worse for the wear except for a curious animal that had inspected the remains lurking inside the food bag Dorrie failed to secure yesterday before her ill-fated hike to Franconia Falls. Wrappers and crumbs of granola lay strewn across the picnic table.

Gail's fingers clenched Mick's strong biceps as she squealed, "Oh no. . .a bear! We had a bear at our site! I just knew something like this would happen."

"More likely a raccoon," Mick said, studying the marks made in the soft soil. "These are not the paw prints of a large mammal."

Dorrie hobbled over to the table and promptly began cleaning up the mess.

"You sure you girls can take care of yourselves?" Mick inquired.

"Yes, we girls can take care of ourselves," Dorrie mimicked.

"Mick, are you sure about leaving?" Gail asked, her hold tightening around his arm. "We can still have a great time. I'll hike with you wherever you want to go!"

Instead of acknowledging the young woman who clung to him, Mick leveled his sights on Dorrie, inquiring once more if he should proceed with his hike as planned.

"Of course, of course," Dorrie told him matter-of-factly.

"We'll probably be leaving the campsite and head for a motel in Conway."

"Guess I'll see you both at the hut at the end of the week, then, that is, if your ankle is up to the climb."

Dorrie wiggled the extremity and nodded. "I think a few days' rest is just what the doctor ordered."

"You take care of yourself," Gail whispered huskily in his ear, tugging on his neck in an attempt to draw him into a farewell kiss. Mick fought against her gesture of good-bye, much to her chagrin. He waved in the direction of Dorrie, ambled off to his car, and soon sped away with car exhaust filtering over the campsite.

Gail's face fell as her brown eyes burned with tears of rejection. "Well, good riddance to him," she spat. "I hope I never see him again."

Dorrie could not help but chuckle. "That's sure a switch after nearly falling over the guy for two solid days now, Gail."

"Well, it's obvious he isn't interested in me anymore." She flounced her shoulder. "C'mon Dorrie, let's get outta this place and back to civilization."

Dorrie groaned under her breath and continued to pack up the site. To Gail, civilization meant a nice hotel with a heated indoor pool and all the comforts of home. Dorrie sighed, forcing herself to relax. If she wanted any time to hike her beloved Mount Washington, she must swallow any indignation and plan for a few days' rest to heal her ankle while allowing Gail the comfort of the hotel. Deep inside, Dorrie could not contain the strange eagerness of seeing Mick once again on the highest summit in the Northeast.

six

The Zealand Trail provided Mick with an easy two-mile jaunt to his first overnight stay of the trip—the Zealand Falls hut, a hiker's cabin perched on a rise overlooking the raging waters of the Zealand and Whitewall River. His muscular legs easily trekked the fairly level terrain and up a hill. By midafternoon, he reached his destination, where he was hailed by the caretakers or "crew" of the hut—two young college-aged men who tended the establishment during the summertime, cooked the evening and morning meals, and provided stimulating conversation to the people who came to visit. It did not take long for Mick to strike up a conversation with the men while assisting with chores around the hut.

Later that afternoon, Mick took a stroll along the edge of the river. He sat down on a large rock perched near the roaring river that eventually dropped over the face of a cliff into a raging waterfall below. He allowed the sights and smells to invade his senses.

Even as he soaked in the rays of sun and inhaled the earthy vapors inherent in the woods surrounding him, he could not shake his thoughts of Dorrie. He remembered vividly her sympathetic embrace on the dark, lonely trail when he confided in her of his painful past. Now as he pitched rocks into the river, he realized how much Dorrie cared about his internal turmoil over his father's injury. Of course his mother cared, and even those in the church once voiced their concern; but here in the midst of these great woods, a woman who knew nothing about him extended a certain compassion unlike anyone he had ever met.

Dorrie had reached out to him with everything she possessed and he had swatted her away like a pesky fly. Deep inside, sensations of guilt and regret nipped at him. Now Dorrie was left to struggle with an injured ankle and a flighty sister. Mick threw the rocks into the river with greater rapidity. The water splashed upward into miniature fountains of spray that soaked his sandals. Here he basked in the great outdoors while Dorrie sat in a cold hotel room, staring at four antiseptic walls, unable to hike the trails she loved with a passion. "Well, I deserve this time alone on the trail," he rationalized, justifying his own fortune. "Haven't I been through a miserable time myself? Don't I deserve this?"

Yet thoughts of Dorrie continued to tug at his heartstrings as he returned to the hut. He recalled her bravery and her determination to hike back down the trail in the dead of night, despite the trials she faced. He compared her strengths with those in her sister, who seemed fearful of everything. He recalled how many common interests they shared, including their love of hiking. He admired Dorrie's tenacity and independent nature, tempered with the humility to accept his help and to admit her errors. The combination of all these characteristics warmed his heart in a strange way, leaving him consumed with thoughts of her, even during the cheery dinner hour at the hut, when the college-aged crew served up huge platters of spaghetti, Italian bread, and bowls of garden salad to the ravenous hikers who paid for food and accommodations.

Mick tried to ignore the flirting of one young woman at his elbow who continually peppered him with questions about the trail, hoping to spark some interest on his part. At times she would jostle his arm with a quick "pardon me!" or perform other antics that left Mick feeling warm under his T-shirt. After the meal had concluded, Mick offered to pitch in with the cleanup in an effort to avoid a confrontation with the young woman hiker, who had gathered with the others on the front porch of the hut. He and the crew talked about biology and their college days as they made short work of the supper dishes. Afterwards, the head caretaker gave Mick back half the fee he had paid for the night's stay.

"We usually offer discounts to those who help with the work," he explained.

Mick stuffed the money into his pocket, thinking of an appropriate gift of thanks he might buy Dorrie whenever he reached civilization again. He stepped outside to be greeted by a cool mountain breeze that caressed his face. The other hikers had long since abandoned the porch area of the hut, leaving it vacant and extremely inviting. Mick sat down on the steps leading up to the hut, taking in all the sights and sounds of the evening. An owl hooted in the distance. The trees appeared veiled in white by the rays of the silvery moon rising in the evening sky. The sounds of the rushing river beyond the grove of trees serenaded the night. Nothing could be more peaceful.

Mick was just beginning to relax the tenseness in his muscles when he heard the sound of soft footsteps approaching from the darkness. A petite figure sat down beside him on the step, cupped a chin in her hand, and sighed longingly.

"Great night, huh?"

Mick turned to see the smiling face of the young woman who had occupied the seat next to him at dinner. As the grin pierced his soul, a cloud lifted, revealing her identity before his stunned eyes. He inhaled a sharp breath before exclaiming in disbelief, "Krysta? I. . .I don't believe it!"

Her smile grew even broader. "Well, it's about time you recognized me, Mick Walters. Took you long enough. And we just saw each other in the hallway at school a month ago. It's a good thing I'm not easily offended."

Mick felt his guard immediately go up and the color drain from his face. He shifted restlessly on the narrow wooden step. So it was Krysta Anderson who had tried desperately to gain his attention during the meal. Her thin, narrow face with high cheekbones and green eyes sent another round of painful memories spinning around within him. . .memories he thought he had suppressed from eighteen months ago.

During that time, Krysta arrived as a substitute teacher at the middle school where he taught. They conversed at length of their love for the great outdoors. For a time they dated. Soon it became obvious to Mick, after several dates, that Krysta desired more out of their relationship than a few simple dates and conversation. For several weeks Mick avoided the inevitable, but eventually he became entranced by her feminine ways and her caring attitude, which eased the pain of his father's disability. The attention he received led to an immoral lifestyle. After a time his guilty conscience burdened him to the point that he finally terminated their relationship, despite her plea that they remain together. Several other times she had tried to rekindle their relationship, but failed. Now she was here in the flesh in the hope of reuniting them once more.

Krysta folded her arms across her chest and gazed at the crescent moon shining above. "So you've become the silent type, I see," she mused. "You didn't say one word at supper this evening."

Mick pretended to scratch an itch on his leg that wasn't there. "Yeah, well, not much to say. But I wouldn't mind knowing what you're doing here, of all places."

"Don't you remember? You and I always discussed taking a wonderful trip to the Whites one day! I asked your friend Jerry about your plans, and he told me your whole itinerary. Unfortunately I had to stay here at the hut an extra day waiting for you. Glad you finally showed up. I thought I'd surprise you and maybe even renew a spark in our relationship, huh?"

Mick bristled at the mere suggestion. "I told you almost

two years ago our relationship was over."

"Oh, c'mon, don't give me that. We're made for each other. You once told me there would never be anyone else, and I still believe it with all my heart." She flung her luxurious auburn hair over her shoulders—hair Mick once loved to run his fingers through. Now he shuddered at the thought and looked down, pretending to examine the sandals fastened to his feet with velcro.

"So where are you headed in the morning?"

"I'm sure Jerry told you that as well," he remarked acidly, angered over the betrayal. He wondered how Krysta manipulated his friend into giving out the information.

Krysta laughed. "Actually he did. You have a very caring friend who thinks like I do. . .that we should be together." She curved a small hand under his elbow and gave a slight squeeze. "Look, my friend Cathy and I are supposed to head back to the parking area in the morning, but I'm sure she'll understand when I tell her I've changed plans. How about a hiking buddy?"

Mick shuddered under the touch of her fingers. He disengaged himself from her grasp and stood quickly to his feet. "No, Krysta," he informed her stoutly. "It's over between us." Memories of Dorrie suddenly washed over him. "Anyway, I have someone else waiting for me at the trail's end."

Krysta frowned and narrowed her eyebrows. "A special someone, huh? Well, isn't that cozy. And you were the one who told me you would lead a chaste and virtuous life. What a liar you turned out to be, Mick Walters." Again, she laughed at the very notion while shaking back her flowing hair.

"She happens to be a virtuous woman," Mick remarked, "which is more than I can say for you."

"Or you!" Krysta fired back with a devilish spark in her eye. "Virtuosity is not in your makeup. I am a witness to that."

The comment cut Mick deep to the core. He staggered

before whirling from Krysta's view and sauntering inside the hut to the bunkroom.

"How can I get you to change your mind?" she called out after him with a teasing tilt to her voice.

The question chased Mick all the way into the bunkhouse. Krysta's inopportune appearance dredged up all the painful memories he thought were dead and buried. *Why did she have to show up here, of all places, just when I was trying to get my life back in order?* He tried to shake off the haunting illustration of the terrible sin plaguing him by concentrating on Dorrie and her strong Christian values. He knew Dorrie was not interested in the flesh like Krysta or even Gail. Dorrie was a woman interested in his heart and soul. *That must be why I'm attracted to her like no one else,* he decided.

Inside the bunkhouse, illuminated by a propane lantern, Mick declined a game of cards offered by the fellow hikers occupying the dwelling. Instead he found an unoccupied bunk and settled in underneath the scratchy wool blanket, hoping to rise at dawn and head out before Krysta awakened the following morning. He lay awake for hours, his hands resting beneath his head, unable to sleep. To squelch the memories of Krysta, he concentrated his thoughts on Dorrie, wondering what she might be doing. He envisioned her sitting helplessly by the tree trunk in the dark woods near the river with her ankle wrapped in a damp bandanna, her miserable face brightening upon his arrival. Mick rolled over on his side and shut his eyes. Again he thought about Dorrie's eagerness to hike the trails and her interest when he shared his experiences in biology. Out of all the women he had known the last few years, no one but Dorrie matched his interests as a key might fit a lock. Even Krysta proved pale in comparison for her interests only fed her flesh and nothing else. Mick frowned as his eyes remained shut. *If only. . . ,* he thought, his hand clenching the pillow under his head, *if only Dorrie wasn't such a fiery Christian with words like thorns of conviction in my soul, there really might be a future for us.*

Mick rose early the next morning in the hopes of starting out on the A to Z Trail, which would take him to another hiker's hut located in Crawford Notch. In the small, modest kitchen of the hut, the head caretaker stood warming a huge kettle of oatmeal sweetened with sliced apples. Sitting at the long wooden table studying a trail map was Krysta. Both glanced up to see Mick as he ventured in and grabbed a spot at the end of the table.

"Well, good morning!" Krysta exclaimed brightly, then moved to a place opposite him.

"Morning," Mick mumbled, hoping to dissuade her interest by his grumpy attitude.

"I was just telling Jeff here how the strap on my pack broke," Krysta went on. "He said he would look at it, but he's pretty busy cooking breakfast. Any chance you could fix it for me?" Her eyelashes fluttered in anticipation. "You always were good with your hands."

Mick ignored the comment and rose quickly out of the seat to pour himself a cup of steaming coffee. Normally he detested coffee, but on a day like today, he felt he needed the strength of the caffeine soaring through his veins. After dousing the liquid with sugar and cream, he returned to his place at the table and Krysta's wide, expectant eyes staring at him. "I'll take a quick look," he decided, slowly stirring the coffee that sent steam rising into his face. He sipped the liquid, made a face, then reached over to the sugar bowl for added sweetener.

Krysta watched his deliberate movements with a small smile. She shrugged back her long hair. "I can't imagine how it broke," she went on. "It's always done so well for me in the past."

Mick took another sip. "What kind of pack is it?"

"Oh, one of those internal frame models. It's not very old,

either. Maybe I'll take it back to the store where I bought it and demand that they refund my money."

Mick placed his broad palms on the wooden table and rose weightily to his feet. "Show me where it is. . .only I don't have much time."

Krysta jumped to her feet and led the way. The pack stood propped up against the side of the hut with one strap hanging loose. Mick bent to observe it, noting the jagged edges as if something or someone had grabbed the strap in its teeth and pulled the nylon apart. "Looks like an animal did this," he observed. "Have you tied your food up at night?"

Krysta knelt down next to him, strands of her auburn hair falling over his shoulder as she observed the cut strap in his hands. She reached out with her fingers, brushing his skin before taking up the torn end of the strap. "I tie it up every night, except of course when I stay at the huts. They have those metal storage bins to hold your food, you know."

Aware of her close proximity, Mick fought to keep his attention focused on the pack. "Well, I might be able to sew it back together, but once you reach civilization, I suggest you go directly to an outdoor shop and have a professional restitch it." He rose with Krysta following him like a puppy as he retrieved a sewing kit from his pack and returned to perform the duty. While he sewed the strap to the pack, Krysta gushed over his handling of the job and how well he manipulated the needle and thread.

"Oh, you're fantastic," she crooned, her head dangling over one shoulder as he worked. Her fingertips brushed back wisps of his blond hair as her breath blew in his ear, sending tremors shooting through him.

"Stop it," he told her sharply.

Krysta was undaunted by the response. "Why? I have a very capable and attractive man assisting me. All I want to do is say thank you. Don't be so testy."

Mick kept his eyes focused on his work. As a strong Christian man before his father's injury, he had committed himself to chastity. Now with his heart hardened to the purposes of God after his father's wound, Mick felt his flesh overpowering and his spirit lacking the strength to ward off Krysta's seductiveness. In her presence he felt himself wavering. His fingers worked quickly, hoping to finish the job and hasten away before he lost all his sensibility.

Finally he tied the last knot and breathed a sigh of relief with the work completed. "There, all set." He glanced around, realizing Krysta had suddenly vanished. Wiping away the sweat that gathered across his brow, Mick rose to his feet, holding Krysta's pack in a powerful grip. He searched around the hut for the young woman as people flocked to the wooden tables, eager for a hearty breakfast before their bodies withstood the rigors of the trail once again. She was nowhere to be found. He finally set the pack down on the porch steps and retreated inside the bunkroom to collect his belongings when Krysta suddenly hopped off a bunk above him like a vulture. Immediately, she flung her arms around his neck.

Mick firmly removed her arms. "What kind of a game are you playing?" he yelled at her laughing face. His feet thumped along the wooden planks of the bunkroom as he gathered up his gear.

"I'm only thanking you for sewing my pack."

"Well, you're not supposed to be in here," he told her flatly, stuffing a shirt and his toothbrush inside a pocket of his pack.

"I most certainly can be," she retorted.

"Look, Krysta, I told you last night. . .I'm not interested in renewing our relationship. It's over. Finished. Done for."

She smiled and shook her head.

Mick thought of praying but decided that was a weak gesture of surrender brought on by a man cornered by his circumstances. He whirled about to avoid her face, only to find her thin arms encircling his waist, hugging him close.

"C'mon Mick," Krysta pleaded. "You're such a great guy. . . strong and good-looking. I know we'll have a great time together, just the two of us, hiking the trails. It'll be like old times again, I just know it."

Mick stood still and silent even as her arms tightened like those of an octopus ready to choke out his life. "No," he again told her, but this time with less resolve.

"Are you sure that's what you want?" her sultry voice whispered.

Mick lurched around suddenly, her face but inches from his. In the dark surroundings of the bunkroom, she appeared demure and appetizing to his weak flesh. He allowed her arms to wrap around his neck, succumbing at last to the temptation of lips that appeared delicious, but in all actuality, were foul and full of poison. A vision of Dorrie flashed through his mind, kneeling in prayer, offering intercession on his behalf. Just as quickly, Mick lurched away from the embrace, the abrupt movement sending Krysta sprawling to the floor. Without another glance, he picked up his pack and fled.

He hiked steadily for hours, his ears acknowledging the soft chuckle in the woods around him and unseen voices that seemed to taunt him through the whisper of the wind in the trees. The hike he endured that day was strenuous, with steep climbs up and down the mountain, yet this did not deter Mick from keeping up a stiff pace. He wanted to place himself as many miles away from Krysta as possible. When he arrived late that afternoon at Crawford Notch, he contemplated staying at the hostel there, but decided against it. Instead, Mick strode out to the bustling highway where cars zoomed by and extended his thumb. He stood patiently waiting for the ride that would take him to Conway and, he hoped, to Dorrie once again.

seven

"I wish you wouldn't go," Dorrie complained as her younger sister modeled her outfit of a short denim miniskirt and rose-colored top, which accentuated her figure, while standing in front of the full-length mirror hanging in the hotel room. With several fingers, Gail fluffed out the curls dancing around her face, then scrutinized her appearance.

"Why not?"

"Because you only met this guy at the pool this afternoon," Dorrie complained. "Who knows what kind of guy he really is." She lay stretched out on the bed, nursing her ankle, which ached after a day of traipsing through the outlet stores with Gail. On the floor lay strewn the shopping bags of items Gail insisted on buying. For her part, Dorrie purchased a better water bottle for use on the hike come Friday and a detailed map outlining the various approaches to Mount Washington and the Lakes of the Clouds hut. Even now the map lay flat before her on the bed while Gail readied herself for a dinner date with a man she had met during a brief swim session at the hotel pool.

"I still think you should be careful, Gail," Dorrie began once again, only to be met by an irritated look on Gail's face.

"There you go again, trying to run my life just because you're older." Gail flounced her shoulder and reached for her lipstick.

"You know that's not true, so why do you say it?" Dorrie answered in more of an irritated voice than she would have liked. "How many times are you willing to get hurt by all these guys of yours before you decide to give up the games?"

"I don't get hurt, I have fun," Gail retorted in defense, now reaching for her perfume, which she spritzed this way and that. "They pay for the dinner and the movie while I sit back and enjoy it all."

The fog of scent drifting over the room sent Dorrie into a sneezing fit. She reached over for the tissue box and promptly blew her nose. "I hope you'll remember not to stay out late tonight," Dorrie told her, throwing the tissue into a nearby wastebasket. "We'll need our sleep. Tomorrow's the highlight of the trip, remember, the hike up Mount Washington."

"Maybe for you, but quite frankly, I've found more interesting things to do." Gail tossed the perfume into her cosmetic bag with an air of haughtiness.

Dorrie puffed in anger but clamped her mouth shut just in time to avoid another flare-up of hostility. A knock came on the door, signaling the arrival of Gail's date. When Gail opened it, a man wearing an expensive leather jacket and cowboy boots greeted her. Dorrie only stared hard, sizing up the guy, hoping and praying he would not take advantage of her little sister tonight.

"Wish me a good time now," Gail said with a laugh before hooking her arm around the elbow the man offered. Her giggles echoed down the hall, even after the door slammed shut.

Dorrie returned to her perch on top of the bed, her eyes drifting to the view of the Presidential mountain range through the hotel window. As she gazed at the beautiful sight of majestic mountains framed in red by the sinking sun, tears formed in her eyes. She wondered if it was possible to meet the challenges still lurking before her, namely, a hard climb up the mountainside, dragging her sister in tow while coping with the effects of a sprained ankle. Wiping the tears from her eyes, Dorrie reached over for her Bible lying on the nightstand and thumbed through the pages until she came to a verse in Psalm 121: *I will lift up mine eyes unto the hills, from whence cometh my help. My help cometh from the Lord which made heaven and earth.* Dorrie knew she must keep her sights focused above, even farther than the mountain peaks looming in the distance, high above into the heavenly realm of God, in whom she could place all her trust. As Dorrie reflected on the Scripture, wisdom slowly sunk into her spirit. Down at her feet and the earthly surroundings, with only the painful reminders of her time spent with Gail and the aching of her ankle, life appeared full of disappointment. Yet when she lifted her eyes to behold the beauty of the distant mountain ranges, life became exciting and awesome, filled with the wonders of God and the realization that He held all of creation and herself in the palm of His hand.

A rumbling in the pit of her stomach alerted Dorrie to the fact she had not eaten much all day. She glanced out the window and noticed a fast-food place just a short distance down the street. While she didn't relish the thought of eating greasy food, neither did she like the idea of eating alone in some fancy place. "Maybe they'll even serve a halfway decent salad," she reminded herself as she slowly rose and ventured to the bathroom. She ran a comb through her bobbed hair, then in an afterthought, dug into her toiletry bag for lipstick and applied a faint trace of rose color across her lips. Shrugging at her appearance, Dorrie turned, whirled her purse off the ground, and strode down the dark hall to the elevator.

While waiting for the elevator doors to part, she offered up a prayer on Gail's behalf. As the older sister, Dorrie felt protective of Gail. Many times in the past, Dorrie found herself in a head-to-head confrontation with one of Gail's numerous boyfriends. One such outburst left Gail in tears, swearing she would never forgive Dorrie for her aggressive stand until they discovered later that year the guy had been arrested for grand larceny. "Sister's intuition" Dorrie always called it. Gail never admitted to her error nor did she thank her sister for her timely intervention, but Dorrie knew her response had been appropriate.

The elevator doors burst open before her. Dorrie walked in and pressed M for the main floor. She unzipped her purse to check the money folded inside her wallet as the elevator hummed and the doors parted upon reaching the destination. With her eyes still focused inside the purse, she walked off the elevator, only to plow headlong into a figure coming from the opposite direction.

The contact stunned Dorrie momentarily. Her hand flew to the tender area on her forehead. "Pardon me. . . ," she began until her eyes focused on the familiar face of Mick with the pack on his back. She stared in surprise. "Mick! What are you doing here?"

A sudden flush marred his sleek, tanned face, giving him a fevered appearance. "I. . .uh. . ."

"What happened to your hike? Is everything okay?"

Flustered by the surprise contact, Mick searched in vain for an explanation but found his mind a complete blank.

"Well look," Dorrie went on, oblivious to his embarrassment, "if you've come for Gail, I'm afraid you're too late."

"I'm too late?" Mick repeated in confusion, furrowing his eyebrows.

"Yup. Sorry to bear bad news, but some other guy already claimed her for the evening."

Mick shook his head. "I didn't come looking for Gail. I. . . uh, actually. . .I came looking for you."

Dorrie stepped back in surprise, nearly colliding into other people walking off the elevator behind her. She led Mick to the lobby, where they found seats in two overstuffed chairs. Her eyes narrowed in puzzlement. "You came looking for me? I don't get it. You must've searched every motel around here, and let me tell you, there's a lot of them."

Mick slid his pack to the floor, again finding himself at a

total loss for words. Instead he toyed with one of the many straps looped through the plastic buckles on his pack.

"Did I do something wrong?" Dorrie asked. "I know I messed up your start time for the hike and all, but. . ."

His face rose to meet hers. "No, no, nothing like that. I. . . well, I was worried about your ankle and all. I wanted to find out how you were getting along."

Dorrie sat upright in her chair with lines of disbelief etched across her features. "You mean you came off the trail just to find out how I'm doing?"

"Something like that."

The two sat in silence for several awkward moments. Neither knew how to approach the other with both paralyzed by the anxiety of the moment. Finally Dorrie said, "Well, that was nice of you, Mick, but as you can see, I'm still on my feet."

"Do you still plan on hiking up Mount Washington tomorrow?" Mick wondered, breathing a sigh of relief at having found a topic of conversation that was not too discomforting. The meeting with Krysta back at the Zealand Falls hut still left his nerves on edge.

"If all goes well and Gail can make it," Dorrie said. "Unfortunately Gail fixed herself up for one hot date tonight, so who knows what kind of shape she'll be in for a major hike." Dorrie added with a chuckle, "I'll probably have to force her up the trail like a bulldozer."

"Gail is definitely not the outdoors type," Mick agreed. "Not like you."

Dorrie stretched out her long legs before her and crossed her ankles in a casual posture, unaware that the movement drew Mick's attention like a magnet. "Yup, I've loved the woods every since I was little. I think it had to do with all those visits to my aunt's place in the Catskill Mountains of New York. I would take little rambles in the woods and such, always on the lookout for some new discovery." Her soft laughter now brought his attention once more to her face. "Yeah, Gail and I are like night and day when it comes to our interests in life. I thought perhaps this little vacation might meld us together, but it's only seemed to separate us even further." Just then, a loud rumbling in her stomach sent Dorrie's hand flying. "Oops, I almost forgot, I was heading out to grab a bite to eat. I'm starved."

"Mind if I join you?" Mick asked. "I haven't eaten hardly anything today."

"Sure. I was gonna grab some fast food down the road." Noting his look of displeasure, Dorrie quickly added, "But if you have a better recommendation, I'm all ears."

Mick rose to his feet. "As a matter of fact, I do. It's a local place, but they serve the best dinner buffet in the Whites. No processed stuff, either. All the food is fresh."

"Hmmm, sounds great!" Dorrie said happily. She pranced her way to the exit of the hotel with Mick lumbering close behind, carrying his pack. "I'm parked right out front," she told him, showing the way to her car. Once there, Dorrie unlocked the trunk and pushed some camping gear aside so he could wedge his internal frame pack among the belongings. With a firm slam of the hatch, she then ambled over to the driver's side.

"I'll drive," Mick offered, pointing to the set of car keys dangling between her thumb and forefinger. "It might be easier if I drive than try to navigate you through Conway at this time of evening."

"Probably better," Dorrie agreed, surrendering her keys to his outstretched hand before slipping into the passenger's seat. "Gail was right about one thing when she said I'm lousy at finding my way around."

Mick flashed her a wide grin that lit his face like beams from the noonday sun. Dorrie swallowed hard and tried not to focus her attention on his handsome features. Instead she occupied herself with the majestic scenery of the mountains framing the bustling community of Conway, New Hampshire. Upon their arrival to the eating establishment, Dorrie squealed like a little girl as she pointed out the restaurant's famous decoration, anchored high on the roof. "Why, look up there, a bear!"

"Sure is." Mick shifted in his seat and crossed his arms. "Now I'll tell you a secret. That, my friend, is a huge grizzly, most dangerous of all predators in the western United States. They shot this particular specimen in Alaska." Mick watched Dorrie's reaction with a great deal of amusement. Her dark brown eyes appeared enormous under a pair of thick, arched eyebrows that now arched even further after this explanation.

"Really?" Dorrie started, then frowned and batted him playfully in the upper arm. "Go on, you're teasing me. That's not a real bear." She again eyed the immense structure, squinting a bit to see in the shadows of the coming twilight. "I think it's made of plaster or something."

Mick snapped his fingers and sighed in mock disappointment as he opened his car door and hurried to assist her. "Thought I got you on that one. You're too smart for me."

Dorrie laughed at the joke as she followed him into the restaurant. The interior of the place was not much to rave about with oblong tables and plastic-coated chairs reminiscent of a high school cafeteria. She was about to say something about the decor until her eyes rested on the bountiful display of food, set to warm in the chafing dishes. Her eyes widened even further when she noticed the chef bring out a real roast turkey and set it before the carving station. "Why look at that! It's real honest to goodness turkey, not that junk made out of congealed broth and fat made to look like turkey breast."

"Hmmm, actually I think it might be made of plaster,"

Mick countered. "It's the decoration for the buffet, you see."

Dorrie again flashed him a look and flushed under the cheerful countenance that now regarded her. The dancing blue eyes and wide grin gave the impression he liked what he saw. Pushing away the thought, Dorrie remarked, "You always seem so serious, I didn't realize you concealed a humorous streak within you, Mister Mick. . .what is your last name?"

"Walters," he told her as a waitress showed them to their seats.

"Walters," she repeated, settling herself into the chair and spreading a paper napkin across her lap. "And where did you say you're from? You probably told me once already, but I've forgotten."

"Cambridge. A suburb of Boston."

"Right, right." Dorrie studied the menu, then tossed it aside. "I'll have one of everything," she announced. "The buffet looks so delicious, I'll probably make a pig out of myself."

"A hiker's prerogative," Mick answered after informing the waitress of their orders. "All hikers make pigs out of themselves at dinner buffets. That's what gives them the energy to climb these ridiculous mountains around here. I'll never forget the humorous story I once read in a manual describing the Appalachian Trail in the White Mountains. Some joker drew a picture of a guy with suction cups on his feet and hands, trying to climb up the face of a sheer rock cliff. Underneath he wrote the caption 'I love the Whites.' He wasn't too far off track about the suction cups, I'll tell you."

Dorrie laughed once again as they both ventured to the massive food bar, promptly filled their plates, then sauntered back to their seats, where the waitress had already placed glasses brimming with iced tea and a small loaf of freshly baked bread. Before digging into the marvelous feast, Dorrie promptly shut her eyes, thanking the Lord in her heart for the food. She offered an additional prayer of thanks for bringing

Mick back, hoping he might be drawn into the presence of God. When she finished her silent prayers, her eyes flicked open to see Mick sitting opposite her, ready to sink his teeth into a hunk of bread slathered with butter. "Okay, you can start," Dorrie told him with a smile.

"Just wanted to make sure God's given His permission before I begin." With great gusto, he began to eat, alternating the bread with huge forkfuls of pasta salad. Dorrie took daintier bites, but managed to clear her plate in record time.

"You're right," Mick sighed in content, resting back in his chair to observe their clean plates. "We are eating like pigs."

"Gail never eats this way," Dorrie confessed after they retrieved a second helping from the buffet. "She likes to impress the guy who's buying by taking tiny bites. Once I actually accompanied her on a date with this one-time boyfriend of hers. I cleaned up my food, then went up for seconds while Gail barely finished half of her first plate before pushing it away and declaring, 'I'm so full! I can't eat another bite.' I felt ridiculous."

Mick picked up his iced tea and gulped down half the contents before placing it on the table before him. "Well, I like to see a woman who eats well. It shows me she's enjoying the date."

Dorrie plunked her fork on her plate, confused by this comment. She had not considered this outing a date, for she was against the whole scheme of dating. Besides the fact, Mick seemed opposed to the many facets of Christianity that she believed. After watching Gail go through the pain of broken relationships month after month, she decided long ago to trust God for the man she would one day marry. Despite the idea passed around in wide circles that one must date to find a prospective husband, Dorrie rationalized if she can trust God for her salvation and her everyday needs, why not trust Him to bring her a husband when the time was right? Now she nervously shifted her feet under the table, wondering if she had made a mistake by going with him to the restaurant. The knot that formed in the pit of her stomach suddenly suppressed her appetite.

Mick noticed the change at once. "Did I say something wrong?"

Dorrie brushed her ill feelings aside while forcing herself to pick up the fork and eat. She shook her head. "So tell me all about your teaching job, just don't get too graphic because we are eating."

Mick relaxed and delved into the various aspects of the teaching profession. "The hardest part is the time," he admitted. "Teaching is a very time-consuming profession. When it's not writing lesson plans, it's dealing with some irate parent, or grading tests, or attending faculty meetings. That's why I look forward to my outings every year in the mountains."

"And do you see your parents much?"

Mick placed his fork on the plate with a decisive clink. "I'd rather not talk about it."

Dorrie inhaled a deep breath. "I. . .I think it would be harder to avoid the problems of your family rather than deal with them head-on." The irritated look in his eyes sent her back-pedaling on the subject. "Of course, you have to do what you feel you must."

"Tell me about your job," he said, steering the conversation quickly away from the topic that bothered him the most.

Dorrie tinkled a spoon inside her glass as she swirled a mixture of artificial sweetener and iced tea around in a whirlpool. "Me? Oh, I'm just a secretary for a big insurance company in New York."

"Where in New York?"

"Downtown Manhattan. Cesspool of the world."

Mick's eyes widened in astonishment. "A single woman like yourself working in the heart of a big city like New York?"

"Well, it's not too bad. I go back and forth with coworkers of mine. I own a townhouse out on Long Island."

"You must make decent money."

Dorrie shrugged. "I make out okay," she admitted, grateful to God for the job that brought her a good income despite the label of a simple secretary. Once she made her move to the big city, it did not take long to realize that executive secretaries for big-named companies could earn almost as much as managers. She attended a business school, spent long hours diligently perfecting her craft, then sought out a position recommended by her school. Dorrie soon landed a job in the insurance company where she now worked. It wasn't long before she found herself in one of the executive positions in the company and able to afford housing out on Long Island instead of the long commute by train from Westchester County, where her family lived.

"So you like working in the Big Apple?"

Dorrie shrugged. "It's okay, I suppose. I like to attend one of those ministry churches near Central Park that reaches out to the gangs and other unfortunates." Dorrie went on to explain the miraculous salvation of a lead gang member by the devout pastor of a church who had a heart for the people of the streets. As she went on to describe the fruit among the depraved of society, she did not notice the strange look that came over Mick's face, nor the way his knees bobbed back and forth beneath the table where they sat.

Each time her voice mentioned the word "gang," it was like a knife stabbing him in the heart. "So this man who outreaches to the gangs is still an active pastor?" Mick asked, fighting the pain of bitterness and sorrow surging through him.

Dorrie nodded. "A truly wonderful man of God. . .really awe-inspiring, especially for those of us who work in the city. It's hard seeing all the corruption that abounds, especially on some of the more notorious New York streets that boast the large porno operations and drug dealers. To have the fortitude to go and witness to these people, that really shows the mind and heart of Christ."

Mick swallowed down the rest of his iced tea in a hard gulp. Unable to control the poison festering in his heart, he lashed out, "Then tell me why God chooses to spare some of these godly men of His but yet leaves others to rot in wheel-chairs like vegetables for the rest of their lives?"

Caught off guard by the deep rage concealed in his words, Dorrie sat still, her thoughts racing. During her discussion of the church in New York, she had forgotten about Mick's father and his crippling wound at the hand of a gang member's pistol. The look on Mick's face sent her spirit quickly hunting for the right words. "Mick," she said softly, "it's the same wicked-ness that dealt the deck against God's elect in the Scriptures. You've read the Book of Acts, I'm sure. Remember the apos-tles of Christ, the faithful men who gave up homes and profes-sions to follow Him, then they were called to preach the Gospel when He ascended to the Father? Do you know how many of those apostles did not end up as martyrs for the sake of the Gospel?"

Mick did not answer but focused his attention on his plate.

"One," Dorrie told him. "Only one lived to be an old man—John, the one who inscribed the visions of Revelation for us on the island of Patmos. God had a purpose for his life. The rest were killed by the sword, crucified, stoned, or killed by some other means. They gave up their lives for the sake of the Gospel. Even Paul says it so clearly, 'For to me, to live is Christ, to die is gain.' For all those who have met death, it is a gain, for they know they live for Christ." Dorrie lowered her voice. "Don't you think to your dad, to live is Christ, even if his body or his brain is dead? He has gained not lost."

Mick felt a fist clench. "Well, I've lost everything," he blurted out. "I lost the man I respected and looked up to all my life. . . ," his words began to choke as they spilled forth, "the one I idolized practically all by life. I used to go with Dad out on the streets when he passed out the tracts to the winos and the prostitutes and the drug dealers. I followed Dad around like he was the greatest thing on earth." Mick bent his head, tears collecting in his eyes. "But now that man doesn't exist anymore. He's gone forever." He swiped up a napkin from off the table and blew his nose.

Watching his pain sent watery tears drifting into her own eyes. "Oh, Mick, you were so right to follow in your dad's footsteps and witness his great love for evangelism. But don't you see? It's not him you're supposed to idolize, but Christ in him, the hope of glory. It's only Christ that allowed your dad the strength to do all those wonderful things he did on the streets. It's Christ we must put our faith and trust in."

Her words drove into him like the sharp quills of a porcupine. Mick's bright red face rose to acknowledge her. "The words are real easy to say, Dorrie. You've never been in my shoes."

Dorrie winced under his stiff rebuke, preparing to venture one of her own, but forcing herself to remain quiet. She must allow God to do the work of healing in his tortured heart. In silence, they rose to their feet. Watching the pain in his movements as Mick lumbered over to the cash register to pay the bill, she knew it would take a miraculous intervention of God for this man to let go of his hurt and to reach out to those who desperately needed him.

eight

Mick and Dorrie endured the journey back to the hotel in a void of silence. After Mick drove the car into the lighted parking area, his hands fell limp in his lap and his head leaned back against the neck rest. Dorrie observed his dejection for a few lingering moments before fumbling for the handle to the door.

At the abrupt movement, Mick glanced over at her.

"I want to turn in early tonight," Dorrie said softly. "Tomorrow's a big day."

His blue eyes regarded her and the stout witness she was, even in the dark interiors of the car. If it was not for her firm faith that convicted him with every blink of her long eyelashes, he would not hesitate to allow a feeling of love to come forth. Yet his own stubbornness prevented him from embracing her or the words she spoke. He only watched in pained silence as she opened the car door and rose to her feet. The knowledge of her departure suddenly yanked a chord within his heart, unleashing emotions within him. Despite her convicting words of the night, Mick did not want her to walk away until they resolved their differences. "Dorrie, wait a minute, will you?"

Dorrie bent down and glanced through the open window of the car. "I can see our conversation really isn't going very far tonight. Why don't we leave it alone?"

Her gentle face and sad eyes wrenched his heart. "I don't like how things are right now," he confessed. "I can see I've upset you. I'm sorry that I just don't bear witness with all the things you've been telling me. You're probably right in saying them, Dorrie, but honestly. . .sometimes I feel I'm too far gone."

This dubious pronouncement sent Dorrie flying back into the passenger seat of the car. Her eyes blazed in a righteous fury. "No, you're not too far gone, Mick Walters, and I won't have you confessing such things. Sure you've been through major heartache in your life. It takes time to get all these things sorted out. God's not in a hurry, but I know He wants you to come back to Him. He understands your hurt more than anyone else." She leaned close to him, staring with a steadfastness directly into his eyes. "You've got to believe this, Mick. You've got to let go of your hurt and reach out to Him." Dorrie sat so intent on these words, she did not even see his hand reach out to cup her cheek and the warmth of a kiss that came calling on her lips. Sensing what had just occurred between them, Dorrie jerked away from his touch. She sat stunned by this tender display.

"I'm sorry," Mick faltered, surprised by his impulsive action during their serious discussion, "but you looked so beautiful just then. Your spirit, your character, and then the look in your eyes. . .I couldn't help it."

Dorrie crossed her arms before her, shaking her head fiercely as she stared out the window at the glow of the streetlights illuminating the hotel parking lot. "I was trying to be serious."

"I know you were. And I can see you care a great deal. . . more than anyone I have ever known." His eyes drifted away as he sat back once again in the driver's seat. "That's why I left the trail, Dorrie. I know you care about me. When you held me on the trail to Franconia Falls, I sensed the compassion and the love in you." He sighed. "I haven't been able to shake off the encounter since."

Dorrie sensed a flush filling her cheeks. "But the reason I did that was to show you how much God cares about you and your situation."

"I know you care, too, Dorrie." He picked up her hand in his. "You're more than just a friend to me. Way more."

Dorrie did not know what to say or think. She desperately wanted to see Mick restored, yet she did not intend to foster any type of relationship with him other than that of a caring friend. Now he appeared willing to cross a line that scared her to death. *I can't possibly have the kind of relationship he wants,* she reasoned silently. *He's from a different world than mine, with a heart imprisoned by the past. After this weekend it will all be over! How can we allow this to go on, only to watch it fall apart once our time here in these mountains is finished?* "Look, Mick," Dorrie finally said, "you know as well as I we aren't meant to be together. You and I, well, we're from different areas, different planets practically. Once our vacations are over, you'll go your way, and I'll go mine. It doesn't make sense to begin a relationship that's bound for the dead zone before it even starts."

The remark stung Mick. He looked over at her with hurt in his eyes. "So you don't think we have a chance, huh?"

Dorrie stared at him, choking back a chuckle within her throat. "Are you kidding? For two people as different as we are. . ." Her words were suddenly interrupted by the scream of tires as a car sped into the parking lot. Gravel flew in every direction. Mick and Dorrie watched wide-eyed as a car door lurched open and some bedraggled figure tumbled out, falling flat onto the road. The door then shut firmly and the car sped away, leaving the unknown person a hopeless mess in the middle of the parking area.

Mick and Dorrie did not hesitate but simultaneously opened their respective car doors and hurried over to the figure sprawled in the road. A disheveled denim skirt and rose-colored top met Dorrie's anguished gaze. "Gail!" she cried, kneeling next to her sister's side.

Breath laced with the overpowering stench of alcohol

reached Dorrie's nostrils. The front of Gail's shirt was smeared with sticky vomit. Gail batted one eye open, then loudly bawled, "Dawrie. . .oh Dawrie. . .he stole my money. . . he. . ."

"Sshh, it's going to be all right," Dorrie told her sister soothingly, brushing back wisps of curly hair tenderly with one hand. She helped Gail to her feet with Mick supporting the other side, and together they managed to assist the wobbly Gail across the parking lot to the hotel entrance, balancing her as her feet stumbled over pebbles and debris.

"Dawrie. . . ," Gail moaned. "Help me!"

Dorrie and Mick struggled her onto an awaiting elevator, then down the corridor to the hotel room. Once inside, Dorrie assisted her sister to the bathroom, where she began to clean her up while Mick waited patiently outside, ready to be of assistance if needed.

"Dawrie. . .I can't believe this happened," Gail continued to sob.

Her tears dampened Dorrie's shirt as she scrubbed her sister's face clean with a washcloth, then assisted her out of the foul-smelling clothing. "Shh, it's going to be okay," Dorrie told her reassuringly.

"Is she all right?" came Mick's concerned voice from behind the closed door.

"I think so," Dorrie answered, "but she's pretty drunk."

"You think she needs to go to the hospital?" Mick wondered.

Dorrie bit her lip, trying to suppress the anguish at the thought of the man raping her poor sister while under the influence of alcohol. "Uh. . .I'll see if she'll talk to me and tell me what happened." As Dorrie worked, Gail sat listless on the toilet, her head slumped over, her hair hanging in curly ringlets around her face. "Gail," Dorrie began softly, kneeling next to her sister, "I have to know something. . .just in case we need to get you to the hospital. Did that guy. . .did he harm you?"

Gail sniffed and shook her head, blowing her nose into a tissue. "No. He. . .he tried." She burst into tears. "He said I couldn't have my purse back unless I did what he said. I told him no. Then I got sick all over his car. . .and he got mad. That's when he left me. . .right there in the road!"

Dorrie closed her eyes, crying tears of relief. Her arms held her sister close, fostering a silent bond between them. "Shhh, it's gonna be okay, Gail. I'm so glad you're safe and sound. Don't you worry about anything."

"But I ruined your trip, Dorrie," Gail finally said. Her eyes, encircled with lines of runny black mascara, stared at Dorrie like a raccoon. "I. . .I should've listened to you. I never listen to anything you say because you're older. Now look what's happened! I ruined everything."

The compassionate side of Dorrie overshadowed any anger she might have otherwise felt toward the foolish girl. "Hey now, we went on this trip to be together. I'm just glad you're okay. You're the only sister I've got, and I'd rather have you more than any ole trip." Dorrie slipped a flowered nightshirt over Gail's tear-stained face and wrestled her arms into the sleeves.

A muffled voice floated out from behind a tissue as Gail croaked, "Dorrie, I want to go home. Please, let's go home, okay? I've had enough. This just isn't going to work out. I know what you wanted to do and everything, but I'm just not cut out for this kind of vacation. I'm sorry."

Dorrie sat back, staring into her sister's bloodshot eyes and runny nose. "You really want this?" she repeated softly, her heart falling into a pit of disappointment. This surprise announcement sealed shut the door for a hike up Mount Washington and the stay at the Lakes of the Clouds hut.

Gail nodded.

Dorrie tried to mask her disappointment. "Well, we'll talk more about it in the morning. Right now, let's get you to bed."

Dorrie fumbled for the door where Mick stood waiting, eager to assist Gail to bed, where she promptly fell into deep sleep. Sighing, Dorrie stared at Gail for a time, watching the rise and fall of her chest, unaware she was trembling until Mick's calm hand found hers. His grip tightened, imparting a strength that relaxed her jitters.

"Is she okay?" Mick whispered.

Dorrie nodded. "The guy didn't rape her, thank God. I. . .I prayed for her after she left, Mick. I. . .I'm so glad I prayed for her." Dorrie closed her eyes, allowing the tears to fall. She didn't resist Mick's strong arms cradling her, soothing away the tears of relief coupled with sadness. "I knew something like this might happen. Somehow I knew. Gail becomes a terrible mess if she has anything to drink, and I didn't trust that dude the moment I laid eyes on him. Gail says he took her money."

"Sounds like we should notify the police."

Dorrie winced with this suggestion. "I don't know if they'll believe her, Mick, with her so drunk. I'd rather wait 'til she wakes up sober in the morning and can tell us the whole story."

Mick thought on this for a few minutes, then said softly, "Guess Mount Washington is off tomorrow?"

Dorrie observed her sister's sleeping form and with a sniff replied, "It looks that way. Gail says she wants to go home." She emitted a long, loud sigh, then walked over to the window, gazing out at the golden glow of the night with the lights of Conway illuminating the streets. In the distance she could see the red and white lights of the observation building on the peak of Mount Washington—the summit where her hopes lie for a glorious ending to her vacation. Now it appeared unattainable. *Why, God?* Dorrie wrestled inside her heart, biting her lip to suppress a wave of bitterness coursing through her. Despite her best efforts, nothing appeared to go right on this vacation. She had to contend with an endless stream of injuries and trials. The peaceful vacation turned out to be no vacation whatsoever, but only a painful lesson of the heart.

A deep sigh next to her alerted Dorrie to the fact that Mick still remained by her side as she gazed at the crystal-clear view outside the hotel window. "Guess you'd better find a place to stay, Mick."

"Already taken care of," he told her. "I got myself a room earlier today when I first arrived."

Dorrie wiped away a stray tear from one cheek. When she turned about, she realized their close proximity and his azure eyes staring down in sympathy. "At least you go on to Mount Washington tomorrow. There's no sense in you forfeiting your stay at the hut. As it is, you've given up a lot of your vacation already."

"I haven't minded in the least," Mick told her, yet Dorrie was too distracted by the events of the day to notice the sincerity in his voice.

"You go on and go," she insisted. "Enjoy it for me, anyway. Maybe one day you can write and tell me what it was like."

Mick stared at her thoughtfully for a few moments, his mind buzzing with possibilities. "Look, there may be a way we can both enjoy Mount Washington while caring for Gail's needs at the same time."

Dorrie shook her head. "That's impossible, Mick. My reservations are already set for tomorrow night. Gail's in no condition to hike. Besides, she's already told me she wants to go home. I'll be driving us back to New York first thing in the morning."

"What if I told you I would foot the money to fly Gail back to New York?"

Dorrie flashed him a look of disbelief. "Are you crazy? Whatever for?"

"I have an idea," he said simply before striding for the door. "I'm going to make a few calls early tomorrow and see what I can come up with." His hand sat poised on the knob as he turned to regard her for a few lingering moments. "I'm going to find out if at least a small part of this vacation can be rescued, Dorrie. Night, now."

Dorrie stood paralyzed, hugging her arms close to her even as the door shut with a firm resolve. "Dear Lord," her voice wavered, "who *is* this man You've suddenly thrust into my life? He rejects You for the hurt in his life, yet he wants to be with me. What will come of all this in the end?"

❧

"Are you sure this isn't a problem?" Gail asked, nursing a pounding headache with a few sips of orange juice. The threesome sat cozily in a booth, enjoying a bit of breakfast before the long drive to the Manchester airport, where Gail would begin her trip home to New York.

"It's all set," Mick assured both Gail and Dorrie. "I've already made the reservations and everything. You'll have to switch planes at Boston, Gail, but it shouldn't be too much trouble. Dorrie has already contacted your mother so she'll be waiting for you at La Guardia around four."

Gail stared at Mick incredulously. "I can't believe you're actually paying for all this." Her eyes focused with great curiosity at both Dorrie and Mick. "Guess you want to spend time with my sister real bad to deal out this kind of cash."

This comment brought a flush to both their cheeks. Mick cleared a frog in his throat and shifted in his seat, glancing in Dorrie's direction. Dorrie pretended to study her plate of scrambled eggs and home fries. This conversation was becoming almost too difficult to handle. When she first learned that Mick had secured a plane ticket for Gail, then arranged to switch their Friday night stay at the hiker hut on Mount Washington to Saturday, she couldn't believe it.

"How did you manage that?" Dorrie gasped in astonishment when Mick shared his secret with her earlier that morning over the telephone from his hotel room.

"Well, the weather outlook for Saturday is pretty poor, so there were several cancellations at the hut. I found you a place inside the overflow bunkroom of the hut, and I'll be staying in the dungeon."

"The dungeon?" Dorrie repeated. "It sounds ominous."

"The hut has several bunks in the basement that they rent out to hikers for a reduced fee," Mick explained. "They call the area the dungeon. I've got a spot reserved."

"But if the weather's going to be bad on Mount Washington, maybe. . . ," Dorrie began, recalling her reading about the severity of summer storms that struck the highest summit in the Northeast. High wind gusts and severe lightning posed the greatest danger to those traversing the exposed ridgeline.

"The weather looks fine until late afternoon," Mick assured her. "They're forecasting some thunder on the mountain, but we should arrive at the hut well ahead of the storm. Sunday is shaping up to be a decent day with some nice views from the summit. What do you think?"

Dorrie wrestled the idea around in her heart, wondering if she dare accompany him on a trip such as this. Did she trust him enough to allow them this length of time alone together on the trail? What if they found themselves thrust into a situation neither could handle? Yet, he had put forth a tremendous amount of effort and money to secure them places at the Lakes of the Clouds hut—the portion of her vacation that Dorrie had eagerly anticipated the moment she arrived at the White Mountains. Her heart wrestled back and forth within her as she contemplated all this. "I guess the next question I ought to be asking is, why go through all this trouble just for me?"

"Because with all the problems you've faced on this trip of yours, you deserve a chance at Mount Washington." Dorrie's silence on the telephone triggered a sigh of puzzlement from Mick on the other end. "Maybe I was wrong. I should've asked your opinion first before arranging all of this, huh?"

Dorrie managed a polite "No, it's a thoughtful gesture, Mick, thanks," despite the doubt assailing her. When she hung up the phone, she only prayed the right decision had been made.

☙

Mick and Dorrie stood side by side waving to Gail as she walked through the doors leading to the sleek commuter that would transport her to Boston and the first leg of her journey home. "Hard to believe she'll soon be in my neck of the woods," Mick commented, watching the hatch slam shut and the small aircraft maneuver about, ready to taxi down the runway.

"That's right, you said you lived in Boston." Dorrie chuckled a bit, attempting to conceal the nervousness welling up inside her. Now she was alone with this man, dependent on him for all the arrangements he had made with their hike and accommodations on Mount Washington. The very thought left Dorrie with an uneasy feeling. She lapsed into a thoughtful silence for most of the trip back to the mountains. Sensing her distance, Mick chose to leave her alone, pondering instead his own questions. Was she angry at him for taking the initiative of flying Gail home? Did she find him too forward in his eagerness to climb the highest mountain in the Presidential Range with her? He considered the possible answers to these and other questions until he could no longer stand the stillness inside the car. "So what's wrong? You having doubts or something?" Mick held his breath, his muscles tensing as he awaited the explanation behind her aloofness.

Dorrie shrugged. "Guilt, maybe. Here I planned a vacation

to be with Gail, who I haven't seen much of lately, and then I end up putting her on a plane and leaving with you."

"I wouldn't feel guilty at all if I were you. She doesn't like the outdoors anyway, and after going through what she did last night, it was the best thing for her."

"Maybe. I hope so."

"Look at it this way, now you can enjoy a hike in peace. I know she was kind of a nuisance to you, especially when you wanted to go on a real hiking trip here in the Whites. There's nothing to hold us back from Mount Washington now."

Dorrie swallowed down a gulp of air as she wrestled with the magnitude of this statement. "Mick, I know you're trying to be helpful and I appreciate it. Believe me, I do want to climb Mount Washington, but I don't know if I should go with you. We've spent a little time together, but quite frankly, I hardly know you."

He raised an eyebrow. "Well, do you think it's wise for you to hike Mount Washington alone with that bad ankle of yours?"

Dorrie flexed the damaged extremity, which had begun to mend after several days of rest. She wondered how the ankle would hold up under the tremendous strain of a steep hike up the rock-strewn trail. "No, it's unwise to hike alone. I found that out the hard way, especially when faced with the prospect of an overnight stay in the middle of the woods with no shelter. But I don't think it's wise for us to be alone the entire weekend, either."

"I see." He focused his concentration on the large semi in front of him on the freeway before directing his eyes toward the side mirror in preparation to pass the massive vehicle. "Guess I should've let you drive your sister back to New York, then."

"Look, I do want to hike Mount Washington. You've been very generous. I'm just not sure about us being together like this."

His fingers gripped the steering wheel of Dorrie's car, which he insisted on driving. "Okay, then let's have it all out in the open, Dorrie. If I were a good Christian man, committed to your God and everything, then would you go with me?"

She paused before saying, "Well, I might consider it. He would understand the Bible's instruction on chastity and I think I could trust him."

Mick's face colored at hearing these words, remembering the encounter with Krysta at the Zealand Falls hut and the kiss spawned by his weak flesh to her seductive ways. He knew his life did not reflect the characteristics Dorrie desired to see in a Christian man. Yet the very idea of Dorrie finding someone else to hike the trails, share joyous laughter, or snuggle close to beside a roaring campfire proved too heart-wrenching. Despite this, he reluctantly answered, "I guess I can see your point. I suppose you have no reason in the world to trust me, seeing as God and I are not on good terms right now. I just thought we could have some fun enjoying what we both love to do." His voice melted away into a silence that echoed his disappointment.

The stillness continued until Mick drove the car up through Franconia Notch. When Dorrie flashed him a look of alarm at the change of route, he calmed her fears by informing her of his plan to retrieve his car. "I figured you'd probably feel better driving yourself around," he stated flatly, his eyes staring straight ahead. "Then you can decide what you want to do with the rest of your stay here without me bothering you anymore."

"Mick. . . ," Dorrie began, then paused as he turned her car into a parking area where his own vehicle rested near the trailhead that led to Zealand Falls. Wordlessly, Mick walked to the rear of the car and hauled out his gear from the trunk before depositing the set of keys into Dorrie's hand.

"Guess this is good-bye, then," Mick said, standing by his

car with his hands jammed into the pockets of his khaki shorts.

Dorrie sensed the turmoil within her. A part of her wanted Mick to stay while the other believed it was right for them to go their separate ways. Inhaling a deep breath, Dorrie thanked him for everything. Again she reiterated the wisdom of going their separate ways.

"Sure," he retorted with a hint of bitterness, whirling about on one foot.

"Mick. . . ," Dorrie began again, then shook her head and retreated to her car. She sat still in the driver's seat for many minutes, even after the sound of Mick's car faded in the distance. The whisper of the wind in the trees now filled her ears. She felt isolated in this vast wilderness surrounding her. Shrugging her shoulders, Dorrie brushed off the pangs of loneliness with determination. "Well, God, it's just You and me once again."

nine

The area known as Pinkham Notch, nestled at the foot of Mount Washington, proved a hiker's domain. Here beneath the awesome peak of the highest mountain in the Northeast, hikers from all walks of life gathered together to plan their treks up to the summit. A lodge, cafeteria, store, and hiker information center all provided the would-be enthusiasts with everything they would need for the steep climb that awaited them.

Dorrie steered her car into the parking area late that Friday afternoon. She found it difficult locating a place to park. With the start of another summer weekend, the crowds in Pinkham Notch were thick like fleas. Finally she managed to find a place at the very end of the large gravel lot, then sat back and sighed. After Mick left in his car, Dorrie decided to go through with her plans to ascend the peak on Saturday, hoping her ankle would hold out until she reached the Lakes of the Clouds hut. She decided to hike the general approach to the hut via the Tuckerman Ravine Trail, which offered her a good climb while being populated by other friendly hikers in case of any mishap along the way. As she rose from the car, her eyes scanned the variety of people milling about, some lugging huge packs on their backs, others talking in groups, dressed in hiking attire and stiff mountain boots. For an instant she caught sight of a guy with blond hair and wearing a red bandanna crossing the parking lot enroute to the main lodge. Her heart leapt wildly within her. Upon closer inspection, she discovered the man wasn't Mick. "Now you're being silly, Dorrie," she chastised herself, locking the doors to the car and heading over to the lodge, where she might obtain information on the hike in the morning and available accommodations in the lodge. "Stop thinking about Mick. He's gone. You neatly severed the relationship. Go on."

As Dorrie passed couples walking arm in arm around the various pathways connecting the rustic buildings, a pang of regret nipped her. *Mick wanted to be with me and I drove him away.* Again she scolded herself for wasting time on her emotions rather than on the nature of the circumstances surrounding the troubled man. "The man hates God, Dorrie. You can't possibly have a relationship with someone who is no longer a Christian. Remember what the Bible says about an unequal yoke."

Dorrie walked into the crowded lobby of the information area. Her senses were assaulted by the sights and sounds of people milling about and announcements blaring over the sound system, alerting people to members of their parties awaiting them at the front entrance. Dorrie ventured up to the desk and inquired if any accommodations were available.

"We have room left in one of the bunkhouses," a guy wearing broad wire-rimmed glasses informed her. "Sleeps four."

"Guess I'll have to take that," Dorrie decided, plunking down her money for one night's stay and breakfast.

The guy took her cash while scrutinizing her thoughtfully for a moment. "You plan on hiking up the mountain tomorrow?"

Dorrie looked up, startled by his question. "Yes. I have reservations at the Lakes hut."

"Hope you plan on leaving early," the guy warned. "There's a cold front coming through tomorrow afternoon. Could get stormy on top of the ridgeline."

"I plan to be up before the rooster crows," Dorrie answered, then quickly left before he asked anything further.

A well-stocked campstore met her curious gaze. Dorrie

walked over to sift through the various equipment and other hiker's paraphernalia, wondering if she might need anything for the trip. Bags of freeze-dried food, matches, flashlights, insect repellent, and other necessities met her eyes. Shelves brimmed with spanking new hiking boots and racks held outdoor clothing. Dorrie gasped at the prices on some of the outdoor clothing, especially the parkas made of a waterproof material that was guaranteed to keep one dry in inclement weather. Dorrie had debated the idea of purchasing such a coat back in New York but settled on a cheaper version of a rain slicker. She hoped it would suffice if the weather turned as nasty as everyone predicted.

Next she investigated the reading material for sale. A variety of hiking guides and manuals were aligned neatly along a rack for her perusal. Picking up one that detailed hikes in her native state of New York, Dorrie inspected the contents with a curious eye, flipping through the glossy pages that described some fascinating walks in the Catskill and Adirondack mountain regions of New York. As she read one section detailing a hike up Slide Mountain, the tallest peak in the Catskills, Dorrie closed her eyes for a moment, reminiscing of her hike during late March a few years back and her surprise at encountering snow that came up to her thighs. Struggling to make it through the cold, snowy drifts, she pondered the idea of giving up on the hike altogether. Somehow she found the strength to continue on, eventually arriving on the rocky summit, where a stunning view awaited her. Certainly the scenery itself was worth it. Dorrie nodded and opened her eyes, focusing on the page inside the manual. There was no doubt in her mind the sheer effort of climbing Mount Washington the next day would yield her similar rewards.

She placed the book on the stand, then walked over to study the huge relief map of Mount Washington. The network of trails appeared like a great spider web, all of which intersected at the primary goal—the sharp pinnacle of Washington's rocky summit. Studying the terrain made of plaster and painted colors to depict the vegetation, Dorrie examined the trail she would take and the position of the Lakes of the Clouds hut, situated on the shoulder of the great mountain. Other visitors also gathered around to point out the geographical features portrayed in the relief.

"But what if the weather gets as bad as they're calling for?" Dorrie overheard a young woman complain to an enthusiastic guy who was obviously trying to sell her on the idea of a weekend excursion.

"We'll be fine. There's plenty of places to stay if the weather gets rough. And I'll be with you, protecting you. I know this region like the back of my hand, honey. Don't worry."

The woman snuggled under the arm offered by the man. Dorrie twisted her face at the display of affection and turned away. When she did, she found herself staring face to face with a familiar set of blue eyes and blond hair.

"Fancy meeting you here."

Stunned by the encounter, Dorrie stood speechless.

Mick now commented with a grin, "Need some protection on the trail, too? I will offer you my services and at a reduced rate."

Dorrie turned away from his eager face. "I. . .I haven't even decided yet if I'm going."

Mick stared at her in amusement. "Oh really? I heard you tell the guy at the information desk you'd be up before the rooster crows. Sounds to me like you're planning on a trip."

Dorrie's face colored. Indignation rose up within her at the very thought of Mick eavesdropping on her plans. She whirled around. "What, were you spying on me or something?"

His features softened. "I'm just concerned that you're

gonna mess yourself up if you try to tackle that trail alone and with all this bad weather coming."

"I appreciate your concern, but I can take care of myself," she answered, walking away. "I have hiked many trails in my lifetime. . .alone, without the need of a guide."

Mick refused to be intimidated by her independent demeanor. "Yeah, and I've witnessed firsthand how you take care of yourself. You think you're ready to conquer the world and then you end up almost breaking your leg at Franconia Falls. You haven't learned the dangers of soloing yet, have you?"

Dorrie bristled, ready to lash back with a comment until she saw the curious faces staring at their disagreement. Instead she marched out of the lodge, conscious of the footsteps plowing the ground behind her. Whirling about, Dorrie fired back, "Mick, leave me alone."

"The truth hurts, doesn't it?"

Seething from the question, Dorrie's mind now buzzed with an assortment of harsh rebukes until she lashed out, "All right, let's talk about truth while we're on the subject. Instead of following me and invading my privacy, why don't you go home to Boston where you're needed? The real truth is that you're so busy being the wayward son who feels sorry for himself, you have no time left to devote to the real needs of your family. They're the ones who need your undivided attention much more than I ever will."

Once Dorrie spoke of the hurt buried within him, Mick jumped back as if he had been struck. Evening shadows muted the rage building across his face before he whirled about in a start and stalked off, his feet pounding the ground with every step he took.

"Dorrie, ole girl, now you've done it," she said sadly, plunking down on a stone step with a great heaviness. "You know Mother's always yelling at you for having the biggest mouth this side of the Mississippi." She knew the sting of her biting words must have felt like a dagger to a man struggling with the pain of his family. "He was just trying to be nice, and look what I did." Despite the truth concealed within her statement, the words would never bring forth the healing and renewal he needed in his life.

Dorrie lay wide awake in her bunk that night, disturbed by the giggles of several girls in the neighboring bunks who refused to settle down. Pushing the tiny switch to illuminate the timepiece on her digital watch, she noted the late hour. *Great*, she thought with a groan, flopping over on her other side. *I'll never get to sleep. Between thoughts of Mick and the racket of those two girls, I'll be lucky to catch a few hours.*

Dorrie tried not to dwell on the reasons for her insomnia but screwed her eyes shut and dwelt on the hikes she had taken over the past few years. She recalled the beauty of the woods, the babble of a rushing brook flowing over the rocks, and the sweet smell of the earth after a rainfall. Often on her rambles she would play praise music through a set of headphones on her Walkman, thinking how perfectly the music fit the scenery around her. Once on the summit of a great peak, she sang loud praises to the Lord, unaware of the other hikers who stared at her strangely. Some even refused to approach the summit but turned and scampered away like frightened mice. Dorrie shrugged, smiled smugly to herself, and picked up her daypack. "Light can't mix with dark," she observed. "Either that or they think I've lost my marbles from dehydration."

As she continued to dwell on these pleasant memories, Dorrie felt herself sinking into the sweetness of sleep until visions of Mick and his concerned face suddenly sent her eyes springing open. She heard his voice reverberating over and over, "I'm just concerned. . .I don't want to see you messing yourself up." Dorrie sighed and turned over once more, the springs to the bunk creaking beneath her shifting weight.

"I wonder if I've made a mistake," she whispered and began to pray for the situation. Dorrie sensed a peace drift over her after the prayer and a relaxing of her tense muscles as sleep finally won over her troubled mind.

᙮

Unbeknown to her, Mick likewise spent the night hours in sleeplessness, contemplating Dorrie's words. While he cared greatly for her, he knew it was pointless to even pursue a relationship with a root of bitterness concerning his father's accident inhabiting his heart. Dorrie's biting words were true. If he could not even care for his own flesh and blood family during the most traumatic times, how could he possibly care adequately for anyone else? He knew a relationship and a subsequent marriage were based upon a union with God and a deep, abiding love that would see the couple through the difficulties inherent in everyday life. Conviction stirred heavily within him. As much as he wanted to be with Dorrie, he knew he must first deal with the obstacles in his path—foremost, his apostasy, and secondly, his indifference toward his family. He could never hope to have Dorrie or anyone else if he did not first overcome the sin that barred Christ from inhabiting his heart. The rest of the night he spent in tearful, conscientious prayer before the Lord of heaven and earth, repenting of his sins and allowing the love of Christ to cleanse his tortured soul.

The next morning Dorrie rose early to repack the items she would need for the hike into her large daypack. In it she placed the usual necessities such as a change of clothing, toiletry articles, water bottles, and a flashlight. She would not need to lug a cumbersome sleeping bag or a great deal of food because the hut would provide her with blankets and meals.

Other hikers were also busy assembling packs for the climb that day up Mount Washington. Many gathered around a scale to weigh in the packs they would carry on their backs for the lengthy journey. By the appearance of the large quantity of gear toted by some hikers, Dorrie decided a few were planning a lengthy walk in the mountains or perhaps even a hike down the famed Appalachian Trail, located in this rough section of the White Mountains.

Dorrie headed into the cafeteria for breakfast and joined a line of hungry hikers eager to delve into the usual fare of eggs and sausage, fresh fruit, juice, and coffee. Balancing the items on a tray, Dorrie slowly entered the seating area, only to hear a voice call out her name. She noticed Mick Walters rise from his seat and wave her over.

Dorrie gulped, almost losing her grip on her tray. *After last night, I thought he would never speak to me again.* Yet there he was, tanned, handsome, with an ever-ready smile poised on his face. Dorrie thought of her prayer last night to God and wondered if this acceptance on Mick's part was His answer.

"Here let me get that," Mick offered, taking the tray from her hands and placing the food down on the table with the efficiency of a waiter in a classy restaurant.

Dorrie tried to hide her discomfort. "Thanks," she mumbled, taking a seat opposite him. From the quantity of food spread out before him, Mick appeared ready to internalize enough nourishment to last a week.

"I decided to make a pig out of myself," he noted rather sheepishly as she stared at the food.

Dorrie could not help but smile, remembering the comment from their first dinner together at the buffet restaurant. She sat down, offered a quick, silent blessing for the food, then picked up a fork to eat.

"Aren't you going to pray?" Mick inquired.

Dorrie glanced up at him in surprise. "I did."

"Oh, I didn't hear you."

"It was the quiet kind," she told him, sprinkling salt and

pepper on her eggs before placing a large forkful in her mouth.

For several minutes they ate in silence while their eyes wandered about the establishment, watching others enjoy their meals or engage in exciting conversation about the events that loomed ahead of them that day. Finally Mick rested his fork on his plate, leaned his elbows on the table, and folded his hands. His blue eyes shone like a clear mountain lake in the bright sunshine as he gently said, "Dorrie, I owe you an apology for last night."

Dorrie almost choked on her eggs. She reached for her orange juice and took a large swallow before sputtering out, "An apology? For what?"

"Well, for spying on you when you were at the information desk, then for rubbing it in about your accident at Franconia Falls." His eyes dropped to his half-eaten food sitting before him. "I'll be perfectly honest. I like being with you, and the thought of you hiking up this mountain alone. . .well. . ." He paused and flushed under the awkwardness of his explanation. "Look, I also wanted to say I think you were right yesterday, telling me I should care more about my family than my hurt. I can see now that I've been pretty selfish these last few years." His eyes rose to meet hers. "You've really helped me see the light."

Dorrie finally set down the glass of orange juice she had been holding. "I'm sorry I spoke out so harshly last night, Mick. I guess I'm just trying to find out God's will in all this . . .if we're meant to be friends or what. I guess I need time to sort it all out."

"Well, I also wanted you to know. . .I made peace with God last night." He rubbed his eyes from fatigue. "I didn't get much sleep, but it was worth it. I had a lot of junk I needed to clear up with Him, especially how I've slipped away from the beliefs I once held onto so strongly."

Dorrie could not help but reach out and grasp his hand in

a tender move that startled him. "You bet it was worth it! Mick. . .I'm so glad to hear this!"

He smiled at her enthusiasm. "Well, it took a young, caring, godly woman by the name of Dorrie to jar my brain and get my thoughts off yours truly. I know I have a long way to go to make up for lost time."

"God is patient, Mick," Dorrie assured him, then dropped his hand when she realized how tightly she had been holding on. "He will help you if you trust Him."

Mick returned to his plate of food, consuming several more bites before saying, "Well, I still don't like the idea of you hiking alone, Dorrie, but since you're so adamant about it, I'll take another route or something. I can always drive over to the trailhead for the Ammonoosuc Ravine Trail, which provides another access to the hut. Maybe I'll still see you at the top, eh?"

Dorrie thought silently on this. Now that Mick had rededicated his life to the Lord, perhaps this was a sign from God that they should ascend the mighty mountain together as a team. "Well, honestly, Mick, you've helped me see a little of the light, too," Dorrie finally admitted. "I was struggling with some pride—wanting to accomplish this hike on my own without any assistance. The accident at Franconia Falls was real embarrassing for me—Miss Hikerette, who has tackled the tall peaks of the Catskills without any problems. But I think it's wisdom to hike in pairs in such rugged terrain, don't you?"

Mick's broad grin and bright eyes sent a crimson tide flooding her cheeks. "I think it's great wisdom, Dorrie."

ten

The sky looming above the majestic peak of Mount Washington lay strewn with high cirrus clouds intermixed with patches of clear blue. The trail before Mick and Dorrie appeared all the more inviting, with the glorious sky framing the tall balsam pines, contrasting the green pine needles against a backdrop of blue and white. As was typical for a Saturday during the summer months, the Tuckerman Ravine Trail was jammed with hikers eager to conquer the steep slopes that comprised Mount Washington. Pausing for a moment to gulp down liquid from their water bottles, Mick and Dorrie savored the invigorating mountain air while silently contemplating the journey that lie ahead. Dorrie was relieved to find her ankle holding up well under the strain of the pounding from the steep ascent that tested every part of her body. Mick offered to carry the heavier items, which eased her burden. The internal frame pack on his back appeared overbearing to Dorrie, but Mick managed it without complaint and with the energy of one used to strenuous activity. Neither conversed much during the hike, with their labored breathing providing needy muscles with adequate oxygen intake during the prolonged exercise. Occasionally they passed fellow hikers taking it slow during the steep climb, while others in better physical shape strode up the mountainside with little or no effort.

The trail leading them to Mount Washington was a rock-strewn pathway, wide enough for an all-terrain vehicle in some parts. As Mick and Dorrie climbed, the trail gradually narrowed and the rocks became larger. At times great boulders rested near the border of the trail, some with flat surfaces that provided a pleasant resting place. Other boulders beckoned Mick with a quick rock climbing adventure. Dorrie watched with some apprehension as Mick rested his pack next to her, then took off using hand- and footholds to climb the rock. When he reached the top, he waved at her from his lofty perch.

Dorrie shielded her eyes from the rays of sun poking through the clouds as she stared up at him. "Who do you think you are, the king of the mountain?" she joked.

Mick laughed. He cupped his hand to his forehead and exclaimed, "What a view! You can see the lodge at Pinkham Notch from here, Dorrie. The cars in the parking lot look like matchboxes. Wanna come on up and take a look? I'll help you."

Dorrie shook her head. "No thanks. I'm thankful my ankle is holding up as well as it is. I sure don't want to take any chances with it now, especially rock climbing."

Mick eased himself back onto solid ground again, where he took the water bottle from Dorrie's outstretched hand. As he drank thirstily, Dorrie could not help but notice the sweat outlining his thick biceps and his crimson face with perspiration trickling down each temple. Observing her out of the corner of his eye, Mick arched an eyebrow and flashed her a grin. Dorrie hastily looked away, a hot flush filling her cheeks as she focused her attention on a tree extending its leafy branches like an umbrella. Hoping to diffuse the embarrassing moment, she commented, "So you looked like you actually knew what you were doing on that rock. Have you rock climbed before?"

"I spent some time with a wilderness adventurers group when I was a young kid. They train you in all sorts of sporting activities, including canoeing, search and rescue, swimming, and rock climbing. I went on to earn a lifesaving certificate in swimming so I could work as a lifeguard at the town pool where I live."

Dorrie remembered Gail's comment claiming that Mick possessed the body of a lifeguard. Somehow the very thought left her uncomfortable. She chastised herself for dwelling so much on flesh rather than on character and promptly thought of Scriptures to ease the tingling sensation now sweeping over her. "Well, I guess that's enough playing for now. We'd better get going if we want to reach the hut before the weather turns bad."

"Right you are," Mick agreed, shrugging on his pack with a grunt and adjusting the hip belt around his waist.

The trail became steeper as they marched onward. Dorrie felt her legs tighten into painful knots, alerting her to the painful realization that she was not in terrific shape. Mick slowed his pace and paused every so often to allow her time to catch up. Struggling with each step, Dorrie resented the way Mick stood watching her progression while gaining all the strength he needed for the next portion of the trail. She required all her energy reserve just to keep up. Gasping for air at the next turn, Dorrie leaned against a tree in frustration and waved her arm. "G. . .go on, Mick, don't wait up for me."

Mick ignored her request and stumbled back down the trail to her side. "No, we agreed to do this together, Dorrie. We can rest as often as you need to."

"Well, as you can see, I'm not Miss Muscle," Dorrie complained, pushing away the water bottle he offered from a side pouch.

"Dorrie, you need the water. Drink it."

"Why aren't you drinking any?"

"I don't need any right now. Besides, we're running a little low. When we reach the Hermit Lake shelter, I'll fill up the water bottles at the spring."

Dorrie sensed her pride firing up within her. "Well, if you're not going to drink, then I won't either."

Mick sighed in exasperation. "Dorrie, this is not a contest to see who is stronger or who can go without water the longest. It's a simple fact of life that men are stronger than women. You don't prove a thing by being stubborn."

"Really now."

"Yes, really. I'm a biology teacher, you know. Men possess a greater muscle mass and a greater volume of blood than women. Why do you think male runners achieve faster race times than women? Why can men lift heavier weights? It's because we're built differently."

"Well, this woman can definitely keep up with you anytime, anywhere," Dorrie informed him, enjoying the prospect of a challenge as she reached down for her pack and flung it onto her back. She began a stiff pace up the trail with Mick following close behind.

"This is ridiculous, Dorrie," he huffed, the bandanna around his head now drenched with sweat. "I thought we were hiking this trail to enjoy ourselves."

"I am enjoying myself," she returned, inhaling several quick breaths as she spoke. "I'm enjoying the prospect of beating you to the lean-to."

Mick increased his pace, hiking stride for stride with her, observing her as her respirations quickened and sweat poured off her face. "You've got to stop this, Dorrie," he protested. "You'll collapse from heat exhaustion if you keep this up."

As they neared the shelter, Dorrie eyed Mick and suddenly thought up a little dramatic episode that might exploit his concern while gaining her an upper hand in the challenge she had created. All of a sudden she feigned a dizzy spell by uttering a terrible moan and placing a hand across her sweaty forehead. "Oh. . .my head! I feel so faint!" She then sank to the ground.

Unaware of the game she played at his expense, Mick rushed to her side. Compassion poured forth in response to her illness. "Dorrie, are you okay? Dorrie? What's wrong? Is it your ankle? What?"

Dorrie opened one eye, soaking in the concerned expression on his face with pleasure. She added a few more moans. "I. . .I can't go on any further, Mick, I just can't. It's hopeless. You're gonna have to carry me all the way back down to Pinkham Notch."

Mick knelt by her side, eyeing this sudden malady in confusion until Dorrie leapt to her feet and began racing along a level section of the trail toward the lean-to.

"Why, of all the. . . !" Mick shouted, grabbing up his pack and dashing after her. When he arrived at the Hermit Lake shelter, Dorrie stood with one shoulder leaning against the side wall, her arms crossed, laughing at him.

"What took you so long?" she mocked good-naturedly. "Weren't you the one who claimed men are stronger and faster than us measly women? I'd say the success of this little experiment proves your theory in error, Mister Science."

Mick frowned and tossed his pack onto the ground before striding up to her. As she stood there with sparkling eyes, crimson cheeks, and cherry red lips grinning at him, he thought she was the most perfect vision of beauty there in the midst of the rugged terrain in the White Mountains. Instead of rebuking her devious antics, he only placed his hands against the stout wooden walls of the structure, pinning her against the lean-to. "So. . .you think you're pretty clever, eh?"

Dorrie's laughter quickly melted away under his tender expression. Before she could react, he was kissing her, enjoying the taste of her salty lips against his own.

"S. . .stop it, Mick," Dorrie sputtered, ducking underneath his arms to escape the encounter. "Please don't do that."

He turned, reached out for her hand, and drew her toward him. Strong arms encircled her in a hearty embrace. "Why?"

Dorrie struggled out of his arms. "Look, I didn't agree to

go on this trip just so you can take advantage of every situation that pops along." Dorrie averted her eyes at his confused look. "This is what I was afraid of," she whispered. "This is the very thing I wanted to avoid."

"I'm sorry, Dorrie," Mick apologized. "I didn't think a harmless little kiss would bother you."

"Well, it does. I promised myself I wouldn't date a man unless I married him. All I needed to see was my sister go through some major heartache before God opened my eyes. Then I did a little reading of my own in the Bible. You remember the story of Isaac and Rebekah, how Abraham sent out his servant with a specific order to find the right bride for his son? The servant asked God to help him find the perfect woman. The Bible says the servant prayed specifically to God that if a woman comes to the well and draws water for himself and his camels, he would know this is the wife God selected for Isaac. Sure enough, Rebekah came and offered water, just as the servant prayed. Isaac and Rebekah never dated, but God divinely brought them together through the servant's prayer."

"Looks like you've spent a lot of time thinking about this."

"Well, when you work in the kind of company I do, surrounded by men eager for relationships, you have to foster principles to live by, then make up your mind to abide by them no matter what."

Mick considered her rationale. "I suppose a majority of us don't have the kind of faith you do," he mused, "but I can see what you're saying. I guess I should be thanking you for warning me about this ahead of time. I didn't realize you felt so strongly about the no-dating rule." Disappointment filtered across his face for he had hoped Dorrie might want to date him. As one who just recently rededicated his own life to the Lord, he felt his faith weak like a newborn and lacking the strength to accept the ultimatum she laid out before him, yet he had little choice in the matter.

An emotional distance was evident when they took up their packs to renew the journey. Preoccupied by his mixed feelings, Mick stayed several paces behind Dorrie as they walked along the narrow trail. He could not deny the strong attraction he held for her, but knew he must temper whatever feelings he possessed. Dorrie held all the cards when it came to having any type of a relationship, and he had to abide by her wishes. He only prayed that God had indeed selected them for a much greater call.

After hiking through a bed of alpine plants on a relatively level portion of the trail, they soon encountered steep talus slopes in a bowl-like configuration that comprised the headwall of Tuckerman Ravine near the summit of Mount Washington. As they gazed at the spectacle before them, Mick pointed out the steep terrain to Dorrie, telling her of the many people who hiked up the trail with skis on their backs, eager for a little downhill practice in the rugged area during the winter. Dorrie's eyes widened in astonishment, trying to imagine the skis laced to someone's back, then the steep march up the hill to a point where one might glide down the snow-covered slope. "There are no ski lifts here, either," she observed. "That's a lot of effort for one quick trip down the mountainside."

"Yeah, but many do it anyway. I for one could never get myself interested in downhill skiing. I'm not much for winter activities. Pam enjoyed downhill skiing, but it was a struggle for me just to put on the skis."

Dorrie now turned to regard him, her eyebrows furrowing in puzzlement. "Pam? Who's Pam?"

Mick noted the cautious tone to her voice and could not help but make the most of the moment. He smiled roguishly. "You mean I never mentioned Pam to you?"

A sinking feeling suddenly overcame Dorrie at the thought

of other women in Mick's life. "No, you never did." Dorrie glanced away, hoping he would not detect her disappointment. "Is she a friend of yours or something?"

"Sometimes my friend, other times my worst enemy."

Dorrie glanced back, unable to comprehend his meaning.

"Pam's my older sister," he finally explained with a slight grin.

Dorrie frowned when she realized she had been misled. Instead of laughing it away as she would have normally done, the play on words grated her. "Well, you might have told me that right from the start, Mick Walters, instead of leading me on." She brushed by him and strode up the trail that climbed steeply to the right of the Tuckerman Bowl.

"Would it have made a difference?" Mick could not help but ask, puffing as he hiked behind her.

"As far as having open, honest communication. . .yes," she answered, breathless from the exercise.

"Well, call it payback time for your little stunt at the Hermit Lake lean-to."

Dorrie could not help but smile as she wiped away the collection of sweat accumulating on her face. Together they watched a bank of fog rise up over the mountainside and spill down into the bowl like great fluffs of cotton candy. "We won't have much of a view from the ridgeline," she noted in disappointment. "All this effort for nothing."

"You're right. The weather's getting worse. We'd better try to keep up a good pace if we're going to beat the storm. The weather's projected to be quite nasty."

Dorrie wasted no time but trudged on, conscious of the growing fatigue in her legs and the twinges of pain in her ankle. The next portion of the trail proved the steepest by far. When Dorrie glanced up, the rocky trail dared her to come master its dizzying heights. Deep gullies from washouts and the numerous rocks made the going all the more treacherous.

"I. . .I'd never make. . .make it up. . .this thing if. . .if I were carrying a loaded pack," she stammered.

Mick was equally breathless in his response. "B. . .be glad we have. . .a place to stay, too. . .once the rain hits."

At the summit of the bowl they continued on, maneuvering through large boulders on a crossover trail. At one point they decided on a lengthy rest by one of the boulders, where Mick hauled off his pack and promptly collapsed onto the ground. Dorrie opened her daypack and fished out food for them to eat. They munched beef jerky and hard cheese while Mick surveyed his map. "We're here," he pointed as Dorrie hovered over his elbow. "I'd say we have about a half mile left to reach the hiker hut, maybe less, and it should be downhill most of the way." He folded the map and turned to acknowledge her, conscious of her warm presence. He felt the tremendous urge at that moment to take her in his arms, hold her close, and kiss her wet lips, moistened from a thirsty encounter with a water bottle. Instead, he reached for her hand, which he grasped tightly in his own. Thankfully she did not draw back. In a soft voice, he said, "You've done a great job on this trip, Dorrie. Ever consider a long-term profession in the area of mountain climbing?"

Dorrie laughed with a sound like bells tinkling in his ear. Her warm breath fanned his face. "Actually I have considered a long-term hike on the Appalachian Trail."

His eyes widened. "Really?"

Dorrie nodded. "When I was a kid, I was fascinated by the thought of spending six months hiking and camping in all those shelters while walking two thousand miles just for the fun of it. I used to buy books on the subject and even went to the headquarters for the trail in the town of Harper's Ferry, West Virginia to check out the possibility."

Mick laughed. "That's funny because I've considered it, too. Unfortunately I would have to take a semester's leave from teaching, and I don't think the school board would think too highly of someone asking for leave time just to traipse around in the woods for six months." His thumb gently stroked her skin, which felt like velvet to the touch.

Dorrie relaxed against a firm boulder positioned behind them and closed her eyes. "Maybe one day," she murmured. "It's a goal I have in life, to walk the Appalachian Trail from Springer Mountain, Georgia all the way to Mount Katahdin in Maine."

Mick again suppressed the deep desire to kiss her as she sat relaxed and at perfect peace in the rocky surroundings above the treeline. He could think of nothing better than spending six months on the Appalachian Trail with this woman beside him. *Not six months*, he told himself. *A lifetime. Even a lifetime with Dorrie would not be enough. God, I know I'm in love with her! Please, somehow, help Dorrie find a love for me.*

eleven

The ridgeline sat completely covered in a thick blanket of fog. Both Mick and Dorrie contemplated the beautiful views they were missing from the rocky slopes as they walked the last leg of the journey to the Lakes of the Clouds hut—a name that proved quite apropos that day. Through a cloudy mist, the exhausted hikers could see an outline of wood and stone comprising the largest of the huts in the White Mountains and nestled beside twin alpine lakes. A few other hikers milled about the establishment when Mick and Dorrie arrived.

"Glad you made it before the storm," the caretaker greeted them after confirming their reservations. He then brought them cups of hot coffee that sent steam swirling into their faces. Dorrie and Mick took seats on the rustic benches inside the hut and helped themselves to the trail mix set out in bowls. "We're receiving news of rather rough weather headed this way," the caretaker said. "The observation tower on the summit says visibility is decreasing and the winds are beginning to pick up."

Dorrie chewed and swallowed a handful of trail mix. "I've heard it said that the peak sometimes receives wind gusts well over one hundred miles per hour."

The caretaker nodded. "Not only that, but Mount Washington holds the record for the strongest wind gust—231 miles per hour back in 1934."

With great eagerness, the young man delved into his favorite topic—meteorology. Mick and Dorrie endured stories of the changing Gulf Stream and sinking troughs until their minds could no longer ingest any more. They politely excused themselves and wandered about the hut, noting the many bunkrooms and the small library of books. Dorrie then followed Mick outside and through a door that led to the basement, nicknamed the dungeon, where hikers could spread out their own sleeping gear on bunks for a modest six-dollar fee. Already the small area was crowded with hiking gear. Mick found one remaining bottom bunk against a far wall, where he took up residence.

"Real cozy down here," Dorrie noted sarcastically. "Looks like the rats would love it."

Mick observed the dark, dank room. "What do you expect for six bucks? This isn't the Hilton."

"That's for sure. Hope you can get some sleep. I don't think I could sleep in a place like this, packed in like sardines. Better you than me."

"I'm glad you have a space in the bunkroom, Dorrie. You should be pretty comfortable."

"If I don't end up with a bunch of chattering girls as room-mates like I did at Pinkham Notch." As Mick unrolled his sleeping bag, Dorrie inquired if he and his older sister got along.

"Well, Pam always thought of me as the proverbial kid brother. Of course I wanted her to play the usual male-oriented activities with me, you know, football in the fall, baseball in the spring, that sort of thing. Pam is four years older than me, so she was always busy with her own activities or playing with her friends."

"But you had friends growing up, didn't you?"

Mick spread out his sleeping bag along the bottom bunk, rested back on his heels, and nodded. "I had a few friends. But I was the son of a street preacher, so that didn't make me popular in high school. You kind of pick up the label of a reli-gious freak for having a father who roams the streets, trying to reach out to the scum of the earth. I didn't mind it, though. I thought Dad was the greatest." Mick lowered his head, suddenly lost in thought. "It will be hard seeing him again, sitting there in a wheelchair, unable to do anything. I. . .I don't know if I'm ready to handle it."

"Just pray and trust God, Mick. That's all you can do."

Mick glanced up at Dorrie and stared into her dark eyes. "I wish you could come with me for moral support, but I guess that's impossible."

Dorrie nodded. She knew there were only a few days left to her vacation, with her boss expecting her back in the office bright and early Tuesday morning, ready to tackle the word processor. "Yes it is. You know I have to be back in the office or the boss will. . ."

"Oh, I understand, Dorrie. This is something I have to do on my own." He found her hand and gripped it soundly. "But thanks for all you've done." He brought the hand to his lips, kissed it gently, then returned the hand to her side. "I hope that wasn't out of line."

"No, it was really sweet, Mick," Dorrie managed to say, thankful the dim surroundings masked the flush creeping up her neck and spilling into her cheeks.

№

Unbeknown to Mick and Dorrie, as they shared these quiet thoughts in the corner of the basement, a shadowy figure watched their interaction through the door at the top of the stairs. The figure wheeled about and vanished once Dorrie announced her need to use the facilities. Mick finished separating out her belongings from his inside the confines of his pack. He did not hear the sound of the intruder venturing back down the stairs and into the room until long fingers clasped his shoulders and a giggle drifted into his ears. Mick lurched away in a start, falling backward onto the hard floor as he stared up into the face of Krysta Anderson.

She laughed at his startled expression. "Hi, Mick!"

Mick's eyes immediately darted to the basement stairs. "Krysta, get out of here," he whispered furiously, watching for Dorrie.

"Why? I paid for my night's stay here, same as you. I can go wherever I want." She glanced about the room. "Dungeon's crowded tonight. I was glad to see you finally made it. The caretaker was kind enough to let me know you'd be here tonight instead of Friday."

"Look, I'm giving you ten seconds to scram before. . ."

She whirled her head around, her eyes blazing. "Before what? Before your new girlfriend finds out who I am?"

"Who you were."

"No, who I am. Look, you can't just snap your fingers and pretend we never happened."

Mick gulped hard, again looking toward the stairs, praying Dorrie would not appear and find them together. He returned his attention to Krysta, who stared back in expectation with her hair cascading over one shoulder in a sea of brown with reddish highlights. "Now look, I won't have you following me like this. I meant what I said back at Zealand hut. Our relationship is over. You may think you need to live in the past, but I won't. I've gotten things right with God. I'm starting with a clean slate."

Krysta burst out laughing. "You've gotten things right with God," she repeated, mocking his words. "Since when has religion ever meant anything to you, Mick Walters? You were supposedly this pious man when we met at school and now you think you're somehow different?" She leaned over, her hair brushing his face. "Well, I know differently. You forget I happen to know everything about you, much more than that new girlfriend of yours does. I know what makes you tick inside. And I also happen to know everything you've been through. You're no different at all, Mister Walters. The quicker someone tells your little girlfriend about us, the better it will be for everyone."

Mick's face reddened with anger. "You just keep quiet. . . I mean it."

Krysta's eyes widened. "Why? Is it because she won't be able to swallow the truth about us? Well, I believe in truth. I think she has a right to know where we stand and that nothing has changed between you and me." Before he could respond, she strode out of the basement with a haughty air to her step.

Mick sat still on the floor, staring hollowly into space, wondering what to do. Dorrie would inevitably find out that the son of a street preacher once lived an immoral life, then what would she think of him? *She'll have nothing more to do with me*, he thought miserably. *Dorrie is a godly woman, a keeper of the word, one who will not even date so she might keep herself unstained. And look at me. Look at what stains me. What am I? I'll be nothing to her but filth.*

A little while later, Dorrie found him still sitting on the floor of the basement, clothed in a dark garment of depression. "What's the matter, Mick? You look like you've seen the devil or something."

"You're close. . . ," he mumbled, unable to meet her concerned expression.

"What's that supposed to mean? Are you sick? Did something happen?"

Mick considered confessing his sin right then but found himself unable to speak the words. Instead he coughed and reached for the water bottle to quench his dry throat, which felt like sandpaper when he swallowed. He recorked the empty bottle and thrust it back into a side pocket of the pack. "I'm all right," he mumbled.

"You're okay my foot. I don't believe you for a minute." Dorrie paused and listened to the swirling wind as it whistled around the eaves of the hut. Rain pelted the walls of the structure with a sound not unlike the shots of a rifle. "Hear the storm? It's a doozy."

"Yeah, a doozy," he repeated, his mind in a daze.

Dorrie frowned, then jumped to her feet. "Well, when you feel like being your old self again, let me know. I'll unpack my stuff then check out the small library of trail guides and nature booklets they have. Come on up when you've recovered."

Mick motioned to her belongings. "There're your things, Dorrie. I didn't know what you would need."

Dorrie stooped to pick up her belongings before giving Mick one more curious glance. "I hope whatever's bothering you, you'll tell me." She strode off, leaving Mick wallowing in a pit of depression.

Upstairs in the bunkroom, Dorrie busied herself with arranging her sleeping area when a woman with long flowing hair ventured inside. She observed Dorrie's movements silently for a few minutes, then stepped forward and said hello.

Dorrie glanced up. "Oh, hi."

"That's a nice daypack you've got there," the woman complimented. "I like the twin pockets in front. Good places to store water bottles."

"That's what I thought, too," Dorrie agreed, glad to have found a woman eager to converse about hiking. For several minutes they talked over equipment and the various trails they had hiked in their past.

"Oh, by the way, I'm Krysta, from Boston," she said.

"I'm Dorrie. . . ," Dorrie began, then paused. "Did you just say Boston?"

"That's right. Actually I live in a suburb of Boston called Cambridge. Ever hear of it?"

Dorrie furrowed her eyebrows. "Isn't that a coincidence. The guy I'm hiking with is from Cambridge, too."

The woman's face became serious. "That's what I want to talk to you about."

Dorrie stared at her. "What do you mean?"

"Dorrie, this guy you're hiking with. . .Mick Walters. . . well, I know him quite well. In fact, he and I were supposed to get married. I had plans all ready for our big day and everything."

Dorrie stood frozen in place, stunned by the announcement. "You can't be serious. You must have this Mick mixed up with someone else."

"I'm afraid not. This is Mick Walters, a science teacher who works at the same school I do. His father lives in a long-term care facility after being shot in the head. I know all about his life, you see."

Dorrie's face fell. A chill coursed through her.

Krysta sniffed, "He's the same one who ditched me, too." She continued on with her tale. "Yeah, we met in the middle school where we both work. I was a substitute teacher and he taught science. We hit it off pretty well, you know? We spent a great time together. He and I decided to get engaged, then poof, he ordered me to leave. I was so hurt by it. I really loved him, you know? I couldn't understand why he would break it off until. . . ," she paused, "I found out he was fooling around with other women behind my back. I couldn't believe he would do such a thing!"

Dorrie stared at the young woman aghast.

Krysta went on. "I asked him if I could please come back. I didn't care about the other women in his life, I only wanted him. I knew in his heart he still loved me. I think he just needed time, you know? I was willing to give him all the time in the world. I wanted to forgive him and get married like we'd planned."

Dorrie's mind was a whirl of confusion. Her hands began to tremble. *This can't be true!* "So you. . .you two were supposed to get married?"

"Of course. I knew we had the chemistry. Everything was

so right." She sniffed once more. "I'm hoping somehow I can turn things around. He knows we need to renew our relationship and go on with our lives." Krysta shook her head, glancing up with satisfaction at the painful expression now filtering across Dorrie's face. Before Dorrie could detect her deception, Krysta immediately lapsed into a sorrowful mood. "I'm so terribly sorry, Dorrie. I can see that Mick never told you any of this, but that's not surprising. He's not one for confessions or keeping a commitment. I hope I haven't ruined your hike or anything."

Dorrie stood to her feet as though she had been stung by a hornet. Her eyes fogged over with angry tears until everything around her became a blur. "No, I'm glad you did tell me before it was too late." Quickly she began stuffing her personal belongings into the daypack.

Krysta stood by, watching her. "What are you doing?"

"I. . .I can't stay here. I can't go on like this, not after what you've told me."

"If you think that's wise. . . ," Krysta began.

"Yes, I do. I'm leaving right now. He'll never see me again."

"I'm so sorry, but I felt you should know what's going on." Krysta gave her one last look, then wheeled about on one foot and left the bunkroom.

Dorrie only shook her head. Her entire body trembled under the weight of this revelation. Angry tears smarted her eyes and ran down her cheeks. *Of all the. . .* , Dorrie thought, shoving her belongings into the daypack as fast as she could, then donning her rain slicker. *I can't believe it. He never told me he was engaged to be married, never told me he ran out on the commitment to be with other women, and now he cozies up to me?* Dorrie thrust her arms through the straps on the pack. *Who does he think I am? Well, I'm getting outta here so fast. I hope I never lay eyes on that man again as long as I live!*

The fierce weather outside matched the torrent of emotion sweeping over Dorrie as she stumbled around blindly. She decided not to venture back down the steep trail through the Tuckerman Ravine, but chose instead the Ammonoosuc Ravine Trail, which would lead her swiftly off the mountain and out of Mick's life forever. Raindrops splattered into her face. Water streamed down the neck of her jacket. How she wished she had purchased a waterproof parka as a stiff wind blew, thoroughly soaking her clothes. Lightning bolts struck the ground all around her. At times the gusts of wind nearly swept her off her feet. "Dorrie, how can you do this?" she moaned to herself. "Because I can't see Mick anymore, not after all this." Mud oozed into the tops of her boots. The trail soon became a river of water gushing down from above as Dorrie slipped and slid along, at times only taking small steps to avoid falling. "I'm a fool," she cried into the rage and fury of the storm all around her. "I'm a fool for allowing him into my life and believing he had changed when all he'll ever be is a selfish, deceptive man."

Dorrie paused, drawing in a deep breath, watching twigs and leaves whirl in a frenzy, mixing with the steady rain. As she stepped off, she felt her ankle twist beneath her. A tremendous gust of wind sent her tumbling uncontrollably down the embankment along with the mud and the water. Branches from the scrub brush tore gaping holes in her slicker. The strap on her daypack broke. Dorrie screamed, trying desperately to grab onto something to break her descent. Her hands reached out wildly, searching for anything, until her head plowed into a large rock and a deep dark void silenced the storm of wind, rain, and turmoil all around her.

❧

Mick soon came to the conclusion that it was better to tell Dorrie about his past mistake rather than have her risk a major confrontation with Krysta. He ventured upstairs and into the main living area of the hut, searching around for her. Instead he found Krysta sitting at the large wooden table, absorbed in a book.

She glanced up at his arrival and smiled. "Hi, Mick. You should see what I've been reading here, all about the species of wildlife found in the White Mountains."

Mick ignored her. He went inside the bunkroom, anticipating Dorrie to be arranging her bunk, but found her absent. He then made a thorough search of every nook and cranny to the hut but could not find her anywhere. *That's strange. I wonder where she could be?*

Krysta cornered Mick inside one of the bunkrooms, her eyes narrowed to sinister slits like that of a cat who had just found a mouse. "What's the matter, Mick?" she asked, fluttering her lashes demurely.

"Nothing."

"You lose something?"

"Well if I did, I wouldn't tell you about it." He tried to sidestep her only to find her barring his path.

"C'mon Mick, don't play so hard to get," Krysta teased. "That's just kid stuff, after all."

Mick sensed the irritation rising up within him. "If you don't mind, I'm looking for my friend."

"Friend, huh? What kind friend is she? One-night stand friend, weekend friend?"

"That's none of your business."

Krysta shrugged and took a dainty step to one side. "You shouldn't be so nasty to me." She wheeled about on one foot. "I may have a hint or two as to where this friend of yours might be hiding." She sauntered away, only to hear the footsteps of Mick following her.

"Where Krysta?"

Krysta stopped and turned, a knowing glimmer in her eye. "We had quite a pleasant conversation, your friend and I. She understands our situation. You and I belong together. It's better this way, believe me. . ."

"Just what is that supposed to mean. . . ," he began until the reality of Krysta's words sunk into him like a fist planted hard into his stomach. He closed his eyes. Dorrie knew about their sinful past.

Krysta shrugged as if his pain was of no consequence. "I would feel sorry for you, Mick, but after all, you ought to be honest about these things. Dorrie needed to leave so we could be together."

His blue eyes widened in alarm. "She left?"

Krysta nodded. "She knows you've already made a commitment. . .to me. So now maybe we can. . ."

"No!" he shouted as he dashed for the door and opened it wide before him. Raindrops stung his face as the wind ruffled his hair. "Dorrie!" he yelled into the blinding swirl of rain. A thick bank of fog marred his vision. *Dorrie couldn't have left in this weather. . .and with her bad ankle to boot.* Mick turned about and grabbed Krysta by the shoulders, startling her. "Tell me right now. Did Dorrie leave the hut?"

"Yes, she left. I already told you."

"When? Tell me when."

"I don't know. . .a half hour maybe. Look, Mick, she doesn't want anything more to do with you. It's the two of us now. Forget about her."

Mick closed his eyes in disbelief. *I can't believe this happened! She's crazy to leave in weather like this.* . . . Suddenly he realized his fault in the situation. *I drove her away by all the secrecy, right out into this destructive storm.* He opened his eyes to acknowledge the severe elements. *There's no time to lose. I must find her quickly before she gets any farther in this storm.* Mick raced through the driving wind to the rear of the hut and clattered down the stairs to the basement room, ignoring the sounds of Krysta following him. He tore open his pack to put on a rain jacket, then jammed gear quickly inside before thrusting the pack onto his shoulders.

"You can't go out there in this, Mick!" Krysta told him, watching his frantic actions. "Are you crazy? Why, it's terrible! You can't even see your hand in front of your face!"

Mick did not respond. All he could think about was Dorrie and her safety. He had to find her, no matter what. Pushing past Krysta, he fled into the depths of the storm that howled mournfully in his ears. *God, how could I have done this to Dorrie? Why wasn't I honest with her? God, please, help me find her!*

twelve

Mick retraced the path back to the junction with the Tuckerman Ravine Trail but found no trace of Dorrie anywhere. The lone hiker he met on the trail only shook his head when Mick asked him if he had seen a woman hiking back down toward Pinkham Notch.

"Hope she's not caught in this," the hiker told him. "As it is, I'm barely gonna make it to the hut myself. The footing is treacherous, I'll tell you."

Mick continued to stumble down the trail and call her name. After a time, he stopped to ponder his next move. Reaching absentmindedly for his water bottle to relieve a nagging thirst, he found the bottle empty, having forgotten to fill it at the hut in his haste to leave. He muttered to himself and unfolded the wrinkled topographical map, wiping away the rain droplets collecting in the crevices to scrutinize the network of trails in the area. It made sense she would venture this way, but the hiker he questioned denied seeing her on the trail. Mick itched a scratch on his damp head of stringy blond hair. Did she decide to continue on to the observation area on the summit of Mount Washington, hoping to find shelter? Or did she hike out by some other route? Either way, Mick knew she could not have traveled very far in this weather.

He climbed back up the trail and hiked toward the Lakes of the Clouds hut once more. Instinctively, his feet turned onto the Ammonoosuc Ravine Trail. Just a short distance from the hut, he noticed a couple making their way up the trail using forked sticks to help stabilize the treacherous footing on rocks now coated with mud. One of the hikers held a bulky object in one hand. As Mick neared, he discovered the man held a daypack that looked strangely familiar. When he asked the two if they had seen a young woman walking alone down the trail, they looked at each other and shook their heads.

"But we found this," the guy said, holding up a daypack with the torn strap. "It was lying in a puddle."

Mick took the pack with shaky fingers and unzipped it. His face paled when he recognized Dorrie's belongings. "It's hers all right. Something's happened. Where did you find this?"

"About a half mile down the trail. But I tell you, you can't go too far in this weather. It's slippery and. . ."

Mick did not wait to hear the rest of the man's warning because he took off down the mud-filled slope, hoping, praying, begging in his heart that Dorrie was all right. Knowing she already suffered from an injured ankle, a bad fall might explain the condition of the daypack found by the hikers. His feet sloshed along the trail. Mud stained his clothing as the water became a swift current around his feet, nearly sweeping him down the steep embankment. Over and over he called Dorrie's name, praying for her faint voice to respond as she once did when he searched for her in the woods near Franconia Falls.

Only the sound of the howling wind and driving rain met his ears. Mick held his hands up before his face to shield him from the mighty tempest, battling both the rage of the storm and the panic in his heart as he continued onward. *I have to find her. . . I must find her. . .* , he repeated over and over in his mind, using the energy within the words to spur him onward.

A colorful object bobbing in a puddle of water down the trail caught his eye. Sloshing through the water, he retrieved a bright red bandanna similar to what Dorrie kept tied to the ring of her daypack. Now he scanned the terrain of rocks and scrub brush all around him. "Dorrie!" he yelled. "Dorrie! Please, oh God. C'mon, answer me!" He stood still, waiting and listening for any sound that might help him locate her whereabouts. He then glanced down at his feet, watching the water part before him to form two distinct paths in the shape of a Y. He noticed off to his right how the water flowed around a bush that appeared trampled by some sort of heavy object. Mick's heart began to race. He followed the trail of destruction until he stumbled upon a figure lying against a rock, covered in mud. "Oh God!" Mick cried, trudging through the brambles until he came to where Dorrie lay unconscious. The wound on her head told him she had smashed it against the rough surface of the rock after a tumble of several hundred feet over the thorny brambles. Blood covered her face. Her clothes were saturated with mud and water. Lifting up her delicate wrist in his massive hand, Mick felt frantically for a pulse and was relieved to find one. He cradled her limp form in his arms, hugging her close as his salty tears mixed with the raindrops that fell on her face. "Dorrie, I'm so sorry, I'm so sorry," he told her over and over. "Please forgive me. Forgive me for not being honest with you." He kissed her bloody cheek. "I love you so much. Don't give up on me now. Please God, let her live."

Her clammy skin and blue lips told him she was dangerously hypothermic. Struggling to reach his pack, he fumbled for a dry sweatshirt tucked inside. He carefully removed the wet slicker from her, placed the sweatshirt gently over her bloodied head, then negotiated her limp arms through the sleeves. Mick winced as a faint trickle of blood ran down one side of her temple from the gash on her head. Removing his own parka, he slipped this over the sweatshirt for added warmth. He realized he must get her out of the elements and into a warm, dry place as quickly as possible. Glancing at his pack and then at Dorrie's unconscious form, he realized he could not manage both on the treacherous journey back to the hut. He abandoned the pack by the rock and hefted Dorrie's unconscious form, draping her across his upper back in a fireman's hold.

With great determination, Mick began the mountainous climb. The weight of Dorrie's form on his upper torso nearly toppled him to the ground. Sweat poured off his brow and he staggered under the load, yet nothing would deter him from seeing his beloved brought to safety. Groaning with the weight he bore, his spirit called on God for strength while he repented of every sin he could think of, including the adulterous affair with Krysta and the neglect of his family. *Please, help me, God,* he pleaded in his heart as he collapsed on the ground. Once more he took the unconscious Dorrie in his arms and found her skin cold. "She. . .she's worsening," he shuddered, rubbing her arms, trying to warm her up. "Gotta. . . gotta get her to a warm, safe place. . .or I'll lose her." Mick fought to keep his fears from consuming him. Summoning a hidden strength left within him, Mick again hoisted her up across his shoulders and slowly, with great effort, covered the rest of the journey in the pouring rain, reaching the hut before he collapsed in complete exhaustion.

છ

Murmuring voices and the smell of hot chicken soup drifting into her nostrils set Dorrie stirring on the cot made up for her in the corner of the dining room. A thick pile of wool blankets covered her. One of the caretakers who was EMT certified opened an eyelid and flashed a piercing light directly into her pupil, temporarily blinding her.

"Hey, what's going on?" Dorrie called out, batting at the light until a terrible pain gripped her. "Ouch, my head!"

The EMT sat back on his heels and sighed in relief. "She's finally awake," he told the anxious residents of the hut who kept a vigil with him.

Dorrie's confused eyes scanned the array of unfamiliar faces hovering over her. Her hand felt the gauze bandage wrapped around her head. "Ouch!" she complained again. "What happened?"

"You took a nasty fall," the EMT told her. "You're suffering from some mild head trauma and hypothermia. Rest easy now. Don't try to move. As soon as the weather clears, we'll transport you off this mountain and to a hospital."

Dorrie tried to sit up until a wave of dizziness overcame her. Reluctantly, she rested her head back on the pillow. "I remember falling," she murmured dreamily. "I couldn't stop myself. The next thing I remember is being here."

"Well, your boyfriend went out after you," the EMT told her. "He should receive a medal for carrying you half a mile up the ravine in this weather. I still don't know how he did it."

Boyfriend? Medal? Dorrie pinched her eyes shut from the pain shooting like electrical currents through her head. He must mean Mick. *Mick went out after me and had to rescue me again.* Dorrie kept her eyes shut as she ruminated on this information. *It would've been his fault if I died out there,* she thought until she pondered the terrible finality of her statement. *Hold on, you almost did die out there. . . . Are you kidding? Mick saved your life. But why?* Exhausted by these rambling thoughts, Dorrie found herself sinking once more into sleep, dreaming of Mick carrying her in his arms through the splendor of heaven's gate.

The EMT tried keeping her in a conscious state, but Dorrie slipped into a sound slumber. He sighed and wiped the sweat from his face, mumbling to the other hikers, "The sooner we get her to the hospital, the better I'll like it."

"H. . .h. . .how is she?" came a trembling voice. The EMT glanced up to find Mick shivering in a wool blanket, his bloodshot eyes staring down in concern.

"Well, she woke up for a minute or two, then went right back off to sleep again. I'll feel better when we can get a rescue team up here and get her checked out at a hospital. She might have suffered trauma inside her brain from the blunt blow."

Mick swallowed hard as he knelt next to her cot. "Did she say anything?"

"Yeah, talked about the fall. At least she's responsive and lucid, which are good signs." Again, the EMT checked her pupillary reaction with his flashlight. "Her pupils are equal and reactive. Wish I could get her to stay awake."

"I'll try and wake her." Mick gently shook Dorrie's arm. "Hey, Dorrie, c'mon now and wake up. It's time to go on our hike, remember? Wake up or you're gonna miss it."

Dorrie's eyelids fluttered as she stirred once again. A firm "too tired, leave me alone" came from her lips.

The EMT looked at Mick and grinned. "Stubborn, isn't she?"

"You're not kidding." He nudged her once more, but she had drifted off to sleep.

"We'll try again later," the EMT decided. "Meanwhile, you'd better get some hot soup in you. You don't look too good, either."

Mick obliged, rising slowly to his feet and shuffling over to a bench, where the caretaker gave him a bowl of soup and crackers to go along with it. For a time Mick allowed the steam to caress his face before he picked up the spoon and began to eat. After a few minutes, Krysta came and sat next to him, her face drawn and her green eyes wide with concern.

"Mick. . . ," she began.

"Leave us alone, Krysta," he told her flatly. "Haven't you done enough damage for one day?"

"That's what I want to talk with you about. I'm really sorry about Dorrie's accident and all. I. . .I never wanted any of this to happen. Please believe me."

"Right. Well, it did happen."

"I know and I'm very sorry." She rose quickly from the bench. "If there's something I can do, anything at all, let me know, okay?"

Mick rested the spoon in the bowl and closed his eyes, overwhelmed by exhaustion and worry. *Dorrie, please be okay. Please, God, please heal her. I. . .I couldn't bear to have another loved one hurt in the mind again.* Waves of anguish coursed over him, remembering his father and the extensive brain damage suffered from the gunshot wound. *Please, God, I will do anything, anything at all. . .only somehow restore Dorrie to me once again.*

Mick and the EMT stayed by Dorrie's side all through the night. Dorrie awoke twice, asking where she was and complaining of a terrible headache, which she described as hammers pounding her head. During each of these occurrences, Mick gently reassured her anxiety while the EMT performed pupillary reaction tests on her eyes.

The next morning, with the storm gone from the mountains, Dorrie was airlifted out via a chopper to the nearest hospital. Mick, on the brink of total exhaustion, accompanied her. He remained at the hospital while Dorrie went through a battery of tests including a CAT scan, X rays, and lab work to determine the extent of her injuries. Mick made himself comfortable on one of the waiting room couches, catching periods of sleep whenever he could. Finally he was allowed in to see her once the physician briefed him on her injuries.

"She's one lucky young woman," he confirmed. "We detected no injury to the brain, but she did receive quite a concussion, so we'll keep her here overnight for observation."

Mick sighed in relief. "So she's gonna be okay?"

The physician nodded as his hands slid into the pockets of his white lab coat. "On X ray we did find a fracture in her right hand. We reduced the fracture and applied a cast. Other than that and the laceration on her scalp, which we sutured, she's in good condition."

Mick nodded, thanking God for this encouraging report.

Now he inhaled a deep breath before walking into Dorrie's room. She sat quietly in the hospital bed with her head elevated, staring out the window when he entered.

"Hi," Mick managed to say, drawing up a chair by her bedside. Dorrie did not acknowledge him but continued in her fixed gaze. Her lack of response unnerved him. "Dorrie, are you okay? Are you in pain?"

Now she turned her head and said stiffly, "Well, you can see I'm not okay." She lifted her arm encased in fiberglass. "What is this thing on my arm?"

"I just saw the doctor. He said you have a broken bone in your hand."

"They had to cast my entire arm for a measly broken bone in my hand?" Dorrie blew out an exasperated sigh. "Great. I'm in big trouble now. How am I supposed to do my work? My boss'll have a fit! He'll probably use this as an excuse to fire me."

"Don't you have any sick leave available?" Mick wondered, trying to keep his voice as gentle as possible.

"A few days, maybe. I'm sure I'll have this thing on more than one week." She closed her eyes in tearful frustration. "I wish I had never taken a vacation in these mountains."

Mick sat still for a few moments, unable to think of the words to say. It was evident to him that Dorrie remained upset over the events on the mountain, events triggered by his own dishonesty. While he cared greatly for the woman lying in the bed before him, he feared she would never care for him.

"So how did I end up here in the hospital?" Dorrie inquired, the question disrupting the depressing thoughts now circulating around Mick's mind.

Mick straightened. "You were taken out by helicopter, Dorrie. The EMT at the hut didn't think it was wise to try to carry you down by stretcher. The trails were a mess after the storm."

"I don't even remember that! You mean I missed my first flight in a helicopter?" Dorrie shifted about in the bed. "Well, it was foolish to go out in that kind of weather. I should have known better, but at that moment, my brain seemed to have turned to mush." She felt the bandage on her head. "Guess I needed a good bump on the head to bring me back into reality. Ouch."

"This was my fault, Dorrie," Mick was quick to tell her. "I. . .I should have been open and honest about Krysta at the onset. I'll admit it, I was a coward. I knew you would look down at me for what I did in the past and. . ."

"So it's true. You were supposed to get married?" Dorrie suddenly interrupted, focusing her dark eyes on him.

Mick seemed startled by the question. "What? No. Krysta and I. . .we were never engaged or anything like that. We talked about an engagement once, but the relationship folded before anything happened. I. . .well, I knew our relationship was wrong. I had abandoned the code I once lived by. At that point, I was pretty miserable with my life. We broke up and haven't been together since."

"Huh. Well, this Krysta whatever told me quite a different version of the whole tale. She said you were quite the womanizer, always dashing off with some lady on your arm, that sort of thing."

Mick gaped in shock. "That's not true, Dorrie. None of that is true. I never had any other girlfriends after we broke up."

"Well, I suppose it doesn't matter now, with our vacations over, Mick." Dorrie closed her eyes. "What a disaster! If God had told me before I started out on this trip with Gail that things would turn out this way, I would've never gone. I'd have remained content to huddle on some crowded beach out on Long Island with everyone else. Gail might have liked it better, too."

"I think it was a good vacation, Dorrie," Mick countered.

Dorrie turned her head and raised her eyebrows. "A good vacation? Are you crazy? Tell me something good that happened on this vacation."

"I met you. . .the most wonderful person there is."

Dorrie opened her mouth wide, prepared to counter the statement, but seeing the look of sincerity in his eyes, decided against it.

Mick continued on. "I met the one person who could open my eyes to my own selfishness and pride. How can I not help but say it was a good vacation? I am not the same man who first came to these mountains."

At that moment, Dorrie remembered the plaque they both viewed in front of the stony image of the Old Man. "And I know I'm not the same, either. I guess both of us have learned something, haven't we?" She then inhaled a deep breath and added, "Guess we can truthfully say, Mick, that in the mountains of New Hampshire, God makes men."

Mick acknowledged her with wide eyes, remembering the inscription on the plaque. "That's right!" he exclaimed. "I'd forgotten about that little saying we found in front of the Old Man of the Mountain. It said something about signs, like a shoemaker puts out a shoe, a dentist a tooth."

"But in the mountains of New Hampshire, God has hung out a sign to show that there He makes men." Dorrie shook her head in wonderment. "How true, Mick. We've both been through that first-hand, haven't we?"

Mick nodded in agreement. "I'll say. When I came here, I was just a selfish kid with eyes on the number-one person in my life, me. Now I have eyes for three. . .God, my family, and. . . ," he hesitated, then picked up her casted extremity in his hand, "a woman named Dorothea."

Dorrie screwed up her face and howled. "Please don't even say that name, Mick! Ugh, I can't believe you remembered it."

Mick laughed softly before becoming serious. "It's the

name of a strong woman, Dorrie, a nurse who served wounded men in the Civil War. I think the name fits you well."

For some reason the comment spurred Dorrie to rest a weary head on his shoulder. This tender display stirred up a hope within Mick that perhaps all was not lost, despite his many mistakes. His finger gently stroked her cheek. "I love you, Dorrie," he whispered.

"Mick. . . ," she began, jerking her head upright to rest once more on the pillow. "I still don't know what to do about us, Mick. I. . .I need time."

"I understand. Take all the time you need, Dorrie. After all that has happened to us, I'll wait as long as I have to."

thirteen

After Dorrie was released from the hospital, Mick suggested they ride a bus back to Pinkham Notch, pick up her car, then he would drive her to her family's home in Westchester County, New York, where she might recover from her harrowing experience. Dorrie protested at first, but Mick would hear none of it, citing her casted extremity and the dizzy spells she suffered since the concussion as reasons enough for a chauffeur.

During the trip home, Dorrie was shocked by her appearance in a mirror at a rest stop on the interstate. When she removed the bandage encircling her head, she found a section of her brown hair had been neatly shaved away, revealing the ugly suture line on her scalp.

Mick became alarmed when Dorrie emerged from the rest room with tears streaming down her face. "What's the matter, Dorrie? Are you in pain?"

"No, I'm a freak!" Dorrie wailed, pointing at her unusual hairstyle. "I look like a punk rock star. Why didn't you tell me? How can I go home like this?" Mick tried to reassure her that she looked beautiful to him, but his words did little to relieve her anxiety. What would her family think? More than likely her mother would either faint when she arrived at the door or have her arrested as a drug addict from the inner city attempting to impersonate her daughter.

Mick burst out laughing when Dorrie confided in him of these reactions, complimenting her great sense of humor. "Keep looking up."

"Yeah, so long as I'm not looking in a mirror," Dorrie grumbled. She played with a piece of loose cotton poking out the front of her cast as the car sped down the freeway toward New York. She then decided to switch subjects rather than dwell on herself. "Are you anxious about seeing my family?"

Mick shrugged. "From what you've been telling me, it should be an interesting encounter. But I'll take it all in stride, as I'm sure you will."

Dorrie sighed as she stared out the window at the Massachusetts countryside. She was unsure of the reception they would receive upon their arrival home. "Gail will probably scream when she sees me," Dorrie commented.

"Out of jealousy?" Mick wondered, giving her a sideways glance.

"Maybe. . .when she sees you. Actually, I was thinking more on the line of my appearance. Gail's pretty persnickety about appearances, so she'll probably tell me how to improve my looks. 'Don't wear your hair that way, Dorrie, wear it like this!' " Dorrie said, mimicking her sister's high-pitched voice to perfection. " 'No, this is a better shade of lipstick for you. And please put on some perfume, will you? You smell like an ox.' "

Mick laughed heartily. "I've got to hand it to you, Dorrie, you sure make the trip go quick. You're better than any entertainer on television. Ever think of becoming a stand-up comedian?"

Dorrie shook her head while her face beamed with pleasure over the compliment. "That's a job I never considered, Mick."

As Dorrie predicted, Gail screamed when they arrived at the modest ranch home in Westchester County. She stared wide-eyed at Dorrie—from the casted arm to the hair shaved from Dorrie's head, baring the red suture line that ran across her glistening white scalp. "You look like you were mugged, Dorrie! What on earth happened?"

"I had an accident," Dorrie told her in exasperation.

"I should say you did! Your face looks perfectly dreadful. Mother will have a fit! C'mon, I know just how to fix you up before Mother comes home from work and sees you." Gail ushered her older sister into her bedroom, where a dresser sat littered with name-brand cosmetics and perfumes. Dorrie managed to slip Mick an 'I told you so' look, which he acknowledged with a grin.

The Shelton family was particularly quiet that evening over dinner. Mother made a few comments, including a quick chastisement for Dorrie's male-oriented feats in the mountains. Dorrie's father proved more sympathetic—giving her hugs of reassurance and asking about her injuries. Later he drew Mick aside and spoke to him for a few minutes while offering a grateful thanks for his care of Dorrie during the traumatic time. When Mick announced he would take a night bus ride back to Boston, Dorrie's father offered to drive him to the bus station. The family then retired to the family room to watch television, allowing Mick and Dorrie a bit of privacy before the scheduled departure. They moseyed on outside and watched fireflies dart by, flashing their bright beacons of light. They slapped at the hungry mosquitos that came calling on their exposed extremities.

"So how are you getting your car back?" Dorrie wondered.

"I'll take another bus up to the Whites in a few weekends and drive it home. It's still at Pinkham Notch in a pretty safe place. I can catch rides with friends in the meantime. I'm not concerned."

They stood in awkward silence, each heart contemplating the whirl of events that transformed them over the past week until they heard the roar of an engine and Dorrie's father backing the car out of the garage.

"Well, Dorrie, guess this is good-bye," Mick finally said.

"Guess so."

Mick sighed and ran a hand through his hair. "I have some difficult things to do when I get back to Boston." He added a bit wistfully, "Wish you were coming with me."

Dorrie chuckled. "I think your parents could do without

seeing a punk rocker, Mick."

He shook his head, then on impulse, gathered her in his arms and cuddled her close to him. "What am I going to do with you?" he teased, then whispered, "Come see me in Boston sometime."

Dorrie disengaged herself from his grasp and shook her head. "I don't think so, Mick. Our meeting was just for a season, you know? God used us in the mountains, but I believe He has other plans for our lives right now."

Mick stared at Dorrie with sorrow evident in his eyes. "I'm not so sure I agree with you about that. . . ," he began.

"Well, I'm sure," Dorrie informed him, patting his arm with her good hand. Her father beeped the car horn. "Go on now. Dad's waiting."

"Guess. . . ," he mumbled, "guess you wouldn't consider kissing me good-bye?"

Dorrie considered his request for a moment, then stood on her toes and planted a swift kiss on his rough cheek before hurrying into the house.

Mick scuffed his feet along the ground to the awaiting car, forcing a smile toward Dorrie's father when he opened the passenger door for him. *Some things just take time,* he reasoned to himself. *Then why do I have this terrible feeling inside I'll never see her again? Dorrie will only be but a passing memory for me, a memory of another life lost to me, like the life I once shared with my father.*

❧

The days and nights proved long for Dorrie following her adventures in the White Mountains. Summer became fall as she continued her job in New York City. The leaves on the trees turned their brilliant shades of red and orange before fluttering gracefully to the ground in the cool autumn breeze. Dorrie occasionally took walks by herself along the sandy beach of Long Island, vacant of the beachcombers and sunbathers with the arrival of cooler weather. An ace wrap swathed her arm after the cast was removed. Her hair had begun to grow back, but Dorrie decided to shorten it in hopes of masking the effect of the damage caused by the fall. Her mother was horrified at the effect, claiming she could not tell from the back whether Dorrie was a man or a woman. The boss at the insurance company where she worked proved reasonable about the whole accident, allowing her less time on the word processor and more involvement with other activities such as filing until she was fully recovered. A new guy in the office named Andy asked her out on a date, but Dorrie refused.

On Sundays, the church near Central Park provided a wonderful inspiration for Dorrie. Watching a few gang members amble in during the middle of the service, Dorrie could not help but think of Mick and his father and all they did to reach the lost in the streets of Boston. At times she would lay awake for hours inside her townhouse on Long Island, thinking about him. Despite her friends and her job in exciting Manhattan, where nothing boring ever happened, Dorrie found herself consumed by thoughts of him.

One day a letter postmarked Boston, Massachusetts arrived in the mail. Dorrie withdrew it from the box and scrutinized the handwriting. "It's from Mick," she breathed, tearing open the envelope to peruse the contents even as her heart began to beat furiously within her.

Dear Dorrie,

Hi! So how goes it in New York City these days? Can you guess who this is? I know you're probably wondering where I got your address. Surprise, surprise! I found an envelope with your address on it inside your car and I kept it. Hope you aren't mad.

I just had to write you and tell you what's been happening.

I hope you're feeling better. I imagine by now you probably have the cast off your arm. Hope your boss didn't rake you over the coals when you returned to your job. I've gone back to teaching science at the middle school. The kids are crazy after their summer vacation. It's hard trying to settle them down so they'll learn something. Sometimes I wonder if I should hire an assistant to help me. If you ever want to change jobs, let me know!

Dorrie shook her head and lifted her eyes for a moment, imagining herself standing next to Mick as he taught the students from large charts displayed at the front of the classroom. The very thought of his rich voice and bright blue eyes addressing the students sent a flush crossing her cheeks. With her hand shaking, she returned to the note.

I wanted you to know that I've been back twice to see my dad. I wish I could say we had a nice visit, but it was very hard. He sits in a chair all day long staring and only yelps when I try to tell him something. He can't feed himself or use the bathroom. Mom insists he's much better, but I find that hard to believe. At least she is very happy to have her 'wayward son' back again. I've gone back to church and received quite a warm welcome. I hope you don't mind, but I shared with the church what happened to us in the mountains. They believe as I do that God's hand was on us, and I think it still is.

Dorrie's hand shook violently. She inhaled a deep breath to steady the tremor.

I know you probably don't want to remember those times in the Whites, but I'll never forget them as long as I live. This may seem strange, but the most tender time I

shared with you was by the rock, in the pouring rain,
when I held you in my arms and told you how much I
loved you. I know you were not conscious at that moment,
but still it remains as vivid to me now as it did then.

Dorrie's hand fell to her side as the last few sentences of
the letter rang in her heart like a bell. The words spoke of a
man desperately in love, yet she did not know what to do
about it. She contemplated answering the letter but somehow
could not bring herself to put the words onto paper. Once
more she decided to trust her future in the capable hands of
God, who never disappointed her. *Lord, if it is Your will that*
Mick and I be brought together, if it will fulfill some great
purpose in both our lives, please make it clear to the both of
us. If it is not Your plan, then please take this man away from
my innermost thoughts and especially from my heart. And
please, do the same with him. Amen.

❧

Time passed and soon the long Columbus Day weekend loomed
before her. Weary of her job in Manhattan and sensing the need
for a new direction in her life, Dorrie decided on a quick getaway and managed to secure a four-day weekend. Thursday
night, Dorrie pondered where she might go. Normally she
would consider a drive home to Westchester County to see her
family, but her traveling bones decided to do something totally
unique. Flipping through the pages of her road atlas, her eyes
focused on Massachusetts and the city of Boston. "Boston. I
could go to Boston. . .maybe see some of the historical sights or
something." She drew in a deep breath, wondering if she dare
surprise Mick with an impromptu visit. Would such a thing be
out of line? She recalled the eagerness in his eyes when he
invited her to come visit him. Perhaps it would even work out
that she could meet his famous street-preaching father in the
long-term care facility.

Having in her possession Mick's address from the envelope that concealed his letter to her, Dorrie plotted out her journey then called her family with her plans. Only her father wished her luck with the trip. "I had a feeling about that young man when he was here, Dorrie girl," her father told her, using an affectionate name for his eldest daughter. "There are very few caring people left in the world. Don't let a good man like that slip away from you now."

Dorrie buried these words of advice deep within her as she selected her outfits for the trip. Perusing her reflection in the mirror, Dorrie wondered what Mick would think of her short hairstyle. As she settled behind the wheel of her trustworthy Mercury early Friday morning, she prayed that Mick had not planned a separate getaway of his own.

The trip went well until she reached the suburbs of Boston. No one told her what a headache Boston was to navigate. She promptly became lost in the complex streets of Cambridge, which all seemed one way with no street signs showing her where to go. Finally Dorrie pulled into Mick's apartment complex after stopping for directions at a gas station. The complex was fairly new, complete with a pool and tennis courts. She drove around, finally locating his building at the end of a cul-de-sac. Dorrie found a space opposite the private entrance to his apartment. She could not steady her jitters as she sat behind the wheel, working up the courage to march up to his door and ring the bell. "What am I doing here anyway?" she questioned aloud. "This is really a crazy thing to do. I hope he doesn't think I want to settle down with him or something. Somehow I have to convince him I'm only here for a friendly visit. . .a quick stopover while I'm touring the sights. I don't want to give him any false impressions." Dorrie finally chastised herself for her cowardliness. In determination, she climbed out of the car, strode up to the door, and rang the doorbell. She waited for thirty seconds, then rang it again.

"Great, he's not home," Dorrie fretted as she walked back to the car. "I should've called and warned him I was coming. He probably decided on a getaway this weekend after all." Through her eyes filled with tears of disappointment, Dorrie noticed her camera sitting beside her in the passenger's seat. She decided if she couldn't see the man in person, she would snap a picture of where he lived to add a bit of nostalgia to her photo album. She grabbed the camera, rose out of the car, and focused for a shot just as a compact car zoomed into the empty parking spot directly in front of her, blocking her view of the building. Dorrie was about ready to ask the driver to move when Mick jumped out of the driver's seat, clasping a two-liter bottle of soda in one hand and a newspaper in the other. He stared at Dorrie and the camera quizzically for a moment or two, his face filled with disbelief, until a curtain suddenly lifted from his eyes. All at once he dropped the soda and the paper on the ground. Dorrie snapped a picture at that instant, laughing at his startled reaction until she heard the sound of the plastic bottle rolling away. She realized then that her sudden appearance had rattled his nerves.

"Oh, Mick, I'm sorry," Dorrie apologized, chasing after the soda bottle as it rolled underneath a parked car. When she emerged with the bottle in hand, Mick was there to take her in his arms.

"Dorrie. . .I can't believe it. You came. You really came." He murmured this fact over and over while holding her close to him, his hands rubbing circles around her back and shoulders.

Dorrie was taken aback by this tender display of affection. She disengaged herself from his arms and meekly handed him the soda bottle she had recovered. "Here's your soda, but I'm afraid your newspaper is gone with the wind."

"Who cares? I have you! Dorrie, you don't know how much I prayed that one day you would come here to see me. I can't believe it."

"Well, it's me. Like my posh hairdo?" Dorrie twirled around. "I grew tired of the punk style I wore a few months ago. This takes all of three seconds to wash and run a comb through. Mother can't tell if I'm a man or a woman, or so she says."

"You look fantastic," he breathed, reaching out his arms only to find Dorrie withdrawing from his embrace. Instead of questioning her standoffish behavior, Mick gestured her to his apartment. "Well, come on in," he told her, "just don't laugh at the mess you see inside. I'm grading papers this weekend."

Dorrie cautiously went inside, standing close by the door as she observed the usual clutter of a typical bachelor pad. Ugly striped curtains adorned a bay window where a withered plant stood. A huge mound of papers lay in disarray on the small dining table. Boxes stood stacked in one corner. The living room was littered with junk food wrappers, soiled cups, hiking magazines, and a weeks' worth of the *Boston Globe*.

"Sorry about the mess," he apologized, bundling up the papers to be recycled and throwing out the rest of the trash into a waste basket. "As you can see, I. . .uh, wasn't expecting company."

"Don't worry about it. I know I came unannounced. I was in the mood to see some of the historic sights and decided as long as I'm here, why not come by and do a little catching up?" Dorrie contemplated sitting on one of two sofas in the living room, but instead maintained her cautious vigil by the door.

Mick noticed her discomfort. "Look, I haven't got a thing in the fridge, so why don't we go out and grab a bite to eat. You like Chinese?"

"Sure," Dorrie said with a smile, relaxing for the first time since her arrival.

"And don't worry. . .we'll just call this a friendly meeting, not a date."

"I appreciate that." Dorrie turned, preparing to head out the door, when she noticed his muddy pack resting against the wall.

A note dangling from a zipper caught her eye. "'Sorry about what happened,'" she read aloud. " 'I hope this makes amends. I'm leaving for the West Coast, got a full-time teaching job. Take care. Krysta.' " Dorrie looked over at Mick questioningly.

"Yeah, I found it on my doorstep shortly after I got back. Krysta was really upset about what happened on the mountain, Dorrie. I guess she found my pack by the rocks and brought it with her when she came home."

"She found your pack?" Dorrie repeated. "I didn't know you lost it."

"Actually I had to leave it at the spot where you were hurt," Mick explained. "I couldn't handle both you and the pack on the trip to the hut."

Dorrie could not believe her ears. "You mean you left an expensive, three-hundred-dollar pack just lying there in mud? What if somebody ripped it off, Mick?"

"Dorrie, I consider you much more precious than any three-hundred-dollar pack," he told her, staring her straight in the eye. "To me, you're worth it. I'd do it all over again if I had to and leave a thousand three-hundred-dollar packs."

Dorrie stood stunned by this display of genuine concern on her behalf. Again her father's words echoed in her thoughts. *There are very few caring people left in this world. Don't let a good man like that slip away from you now.* "Wow, that's really. . .well, quite touching."

"C'mon," he gestured. "There's a restaurant about five blocks away. I think you'll like it."

Dorrie followed him out the door yet remained bewildered by all that she had seen and heard. Perhaps God was indeed trying to lead her in this matter of the heart, but once again, she found her questions and doubts blocking the way. How would she know His will for sure? There must be a way to discover if her path in life was indeed leading her straight to Mick Walters.

fourteen

Dorrie savored every drop of the delicious green tea served in tiny cups at the Chinese restaurant, then set to work on her eggroll as Mick filled her in on his classes for the new term. "They're a rowdy bunch," he confessed, dipping his roll into a dish of hot mustard. "Every new group seems to test me as the teacher, trying to decide if I'm a pushover."

"Are you?" Dorrie wondered, wiping off her lips with a napkin.

Mick winked his eye. "Now that depends on who's in my company."

Dorrie had not meant to make a leading statement and now found herself blushing. She averted her gaze and tried concentrating on eating her eggroll, but with much less enjoyment.

"Do you think I'm a pushover?" he asked.

Dorrie laughed. "Definitely not. Once your mind is made up, not much can change it. A pushover goes wherever the wind blows. Mick is one who follows his heart." Again, Dorrie found herself flustered when his blue eyes softened under the glow of the light glimmering over their booth.

Mick laid down his eggroll and reached for her hand, which she instinctively placed on her lap. "Dorrie, I've tried so many times to tell you what's going on in my heart. . . ," he began.

"I know. Unfortunately, it takes two to tango. Mine is only full of questions. You can't make a decision when all you have is questions."

"If you have a question, I'll do my best to answer it," he told her. "I know I made a big mistake by not telling you everything about my life. As far as I know, there are no more skeletons left in the closet."

"I've forgiven you for the past. My question really has to do with God's will for my life. I want to be sure it's His will and not some wild emotional whim, don't you?"

"I know His will," Mick said defensively, "and it is no emotional whim. I've tried many times to tell you, Dorrie, but you won't stop long enough to listen."

Dorrie's mouth went dry. She reached for her glass of ice water, gulping down the cool liquid before replacing it on the table. *This is not going well at all,* she thought to herself.

He sensed the restlessness stirring at the table. "Look, forget about it for the time being. I wanted to tell you I'm planning to visit my dad tomorrow. You interested in going with me? You can meet my mother afterwards; she's hosting a picnic at a nearby park for the church."

The sudden change of topic threw Dorrie into a confusing spin. "Well, yeah, sure, I guess so. I mean, yes. I really do want to meet your father and the picnic sounds very nice."

"I've already told Mom about you and what happened during the vacation. She thinks you're the living end since you rescued her wayward son from his mountain of sin."

"Well, did you tell her you actually performed the hands-on rescue on Mount Washington?" Dorrie wondered.

"Yeah, but that's beside the point. To my mom, who's been praying for me solidly since Dad's accident, it's the best news she's had in a long time." He then inhaled a deep breath. "Dorrie, I want you to know I've been thinking a lot about us. I think we have a lot in common. We're right for each other, I know it. I would really like to give Mom more good news tomorrow if I could. . ."

Sensing what he was about to say, Dorrie shook her head and rose quickly to her feet. "I didn't come all the way here to Boston to get backed into a corner, Mick Walters. The answer's no."

Mick also came to his feet, even as Dorrie fumbled to retrieve her coat thrown over the back of her chair. "Please wait, Dorrie. I won't mention it anymore. It's just. . .I love you so much. I don't want you to slip away from me."

"Please, Mick, no more. What time should I be ready to see your father?"

"I'll leave around noon," he mumbled, sitting down hard in his seat, nearly upsetting his water glass.

"Okay, I'll come by your place around noon." Dorrie observed his dejection as he stared into his plate of uneaten food. With mechanical movements, he pulled out a few bills from his wallet, rose, and walked over to pay the cashier. Dorrie stood waiting as he paid the check, then followed him to his car without comment. When Mick pulled into the parking lot of the apartment where Dorrie's car sat, he turned and eyed her.

"Dorrie, I have just one question to ask you. The truth. Why did you come all the way here to see me?"

Dorrie's eyes widened. She felt herself shrinking under his penetrating glare. In a shaky voice, she said, "Why. . .a f. . . friendly visit, pure and simple."

"A friendly visit, pure and simple, huh?" Mick sighed. "Okay, I'll take your word for it."

Never did Dorrie endure such emotional turmoil over a man before in her life. She spent the remainder of the evening in her motel room thinking about the conversation. She knew Mick was poised to ask for her hand in marriage, yet the very thought sent shivers racing down her spine. "I can't marry him, God," she told her unseen Friend and constant Companion. "I have a life in New York, he has a life here in Boston. In fact, he's only now beginning to get his life back together. How can I make him see that a lifetime commitment just isn't right for two people as different as we are." Dorrie flipped over on her side, tossing a white pillow over her head. "Why can't we just be friends. . .two friends that like to hike and eat out and share good times? Why do we have to become entangled in this love connection, which only causes heartache and grief?" These questions reflected the doubt burdening her heart. They were questions she could not make Mick understand, for he was too wrapped up in his own emotion to even consider them.

❧

The motel phone rang the next morning just as Dorrie emerged from the shower with a towel wrapped like a turban around her head. She nearly knocked over her suitcase in her haste to pick up the phone and offered a breathless hello.

"You sound like you just ran the hundred-meter dash," Mick joked through the receiver.

"Just about."

"Well, look, I make some pretty wild blueberry pancakes. You interested in a brunch over at my place? Then we can leave from here to visit my dad."

Dorrie hesitated until the growling of her stomach over-shadowed any resistance to the idea. "Sure, that sounds great."

A sigh of relief drifted over the phone. "Look, I also want to apologize for putting you on the spot last night in the restaurant. It's fine with me if we just stay friends. The Lord knows we can use friends nowadays."

Now it was Dorrie's turn to sigh, thanking God in her heart for his decision. "Great, Mick. See you in about half an hour."

"All right then. See you." The phone clicked in her ear to be replaced by the buzz of the dial tone. As Dorrie returned the receiver to the cradle, she smiled to herself, then skipped over to the sink to apply her makeup and blow-dry her damp hair. "Thank goodness," she breathed.

❧

The smell of pancakes wafted in the air when Mick, clad in a chef's apron with a spatula in one hand, greeted her at the door. Dorrie could not help but giggle at his attire. As she strode into the kitchen to observe the batch of crisp pancakes he had prepared, she nodded her head in satisfaction. "They look wonderful, Mick. I thought you once said guys couldn't cook."

"Well, pancakes is about the only thing I *can* cook," he confessed, using his spatula to flip over the next batch. Above him the microwave whined, followed by a buzzer. "Would you mind getting that? It's maple syrup."

Dorrie was more than impressed when she removed a small pitcher of real maple syrup and placed it on the table. Mick had taken great pains to set the table with matching dishes and silverware. As she gazed about the apartment now transformed into decent living quarters, she complimented his hard work. "This is really something, Mick," she observed, sitting down happily at the table as he placed a huge platter of pancakes before her. Sausage links sat in another dish. "Yum, yum, looks scrumptious."

Mick sat down opposite her, bent his head, and offered a simple blessing for the meal—the first words of prayer Dorrie ever heard him utter. A warmth flowed through her heart when she thought of the great transformation that had occurred within him. When she first met Mick in the White Mountains, he was an embittered man who could not stand the idea of prayer or someone offering prayer on his behalf. Now he spoke the words with a confidence and ease as if praying was the most natural thing in the world.

He rose and served her pancakes and sausage, then offered her the warm pitcher of syrup. For a moment Dorrie could only stare at the food on her plate, thinking of the love and care that went into the preparation of a simple meal. The very thought sent tears welling up in her eyes.

Mick watched her reactions thoughtfully. "Are you okay, Dorrie?"

She jerked herself upright and wiped the tears away with the corner of a paper napkin. "Oh sure, Mick, sure."

He gestured with his fork. "I hope you like sausages. I think I remember you eating them back in the cafeteria at Pinkham Notch."

"Yeah," she responded absentmindedly.

Mick did not know what to make of her strange reaction. He ate silently, yet cast curious glances every so often. Dorrie also consumed the breakfast without offering conversation, immersed in deep thought. Finally, she broke the silence by asking Mick about his father's condition.

"He looked pretty bad to me last time I was over there. The visit didn't last too long. I told him about myself and how I had gotten right with the Lord. Sometimes it seems he is listening to me, but I can't tell. He says a strange word like 'yow' or something like that. Then he howls and shifts around in his chair." Mick shrugged helplessly. "I didn't know what to do. I told him I loved him and everything, then I left."

"And you say he can't do anything for himself?"

Mick drank some orange juice before continuing. "The nurses leave him dressed in a hospital gown because he can't use the. . .well, you know, the bathroom and all. He has problems sitting up, so they have him in some type of reclining chair, a lounge chair I think my mom called it." He blinked before adding softly, "I wish you could know him the way I used to know him, Dorrie."

Dorrie offered a compassionate smile. "Well, if he is anything like his son, I'm sure he must be a great person."

Mick's face softened upon hearing this uplifting comment, then he returned to his stack of pancakes. After swallowing several mouthfuls, he said, "You always seem to know the right words at the right time."

Dorrie smiled as she carried her dirty dishes over to the sink. Rolling up the sleeves to her shirt, she proceeded to wash them while Mick carried the rest of the plates over and deposited them into the soapy water. For a time Mick stood and watched her work. He wanted to make some witty comment, such as how perfectly she fit in with the surroundings, but decided against it. Knowing Dorrie the way he did, she would undoubtedly think the comment presumptuous and overbearing. He sighed and retrieved a dish towel to wipe up the dishes that now sparkled in the drainer. How he agonized over the woman standing before him. Dorrie stood so close to him but she seemed so far away at the same time—as if it would take a long, arduous journey up a steep mountain just to reach her heart. He enjoyed her warm presence and found himself fighting off the nagging urge to hold her. He had made a commitment on the phone to remain friends. Now it was his responsibility to keep his word despite the longing in his heart.

Just before departing, Dorrie again noticed the stack of boxes piled high in the corner of his apartment. She inquired if he was moving into another place.

"No," Mick responded, striding over to one of the open boxes and withdrawing a pamphlet. "I ordered these when I came back from the mountains." He handed one to her.

Dorrie took the booklet from his outstretched hand and perused the contents. "Why, this is a tract."

"These are the same tracts my dad used to give out on the streets before he was shot," Mick explained.

Dorrie's eyes widened as she stared first at the tract, then at Mick. "Are you thinking of going back to the streets?"

He nodded. "I'm considering it. Right now I'm in the midst of taking an evangelism class at my mom's church. One can get pretty rusty in the things of God after backsliding for two or more years."

"Wow, this is wonderful, Mick! What a great mission field. I can't tell you how much I admire the work that goes on among the gangs in the streets of New York. They are a group right here in America in desperate need of missionaries willing to reach them."

"Yeah, well, I decided if my dad can't do the work anymore, someone oughtta be willing to take up where he left off." Mick took the tract from her and placed it with the others inside the box.

"Have you told your dad what you're doing?" Dorrie asked.

"Told my dad?" Mick snorted as if the suggestion seemed ludicrous. "He doesn't understand anything I tell him, Dorrie. I don't even think he knows who I am. Mom always tells me he knows. She can see it in his eye or hear it when he yells. I think it's just wishful thinking on her part, to be honest."

Dorrie retrieved another tract. "Well, let's tell him about your call and see how he responds, Mick. It can't do any harm, can it?"

"I suppose not."

He held open the door for her as she ventured out, clutching the booklet tight in her hand. Warm, bright sunshine greeted them. Colored leaves swirled around before finding resting places in the grass or on the blacktop of the parking area.

"This is going to be a glorious day, Mick," Dorrie declared, settling down in the passenger's seat of his car. "I can just feel it."

So long as you're with me, he thought. *We could have a glorious life, too.* But he kept the comment tucked away inside where it belonged.

ta

The long-term care facility where Mick's father lived was filled with the scent of antiseptic, freshly starched sheets, and other odors Dorrie could not identify. She followed Mick to the elevator, conscious of her own anxiety. Mick likewise appeared nervous about the visit. His neck muscles were taut and his finger shaking as he pressed the button labeled three. Neither of them spoke a word as the elevator beeped and they stepped off to be greeted by a terrible noise echoing down the corridor.

Mick sighed. "That's Dad you hear," he whispered to Dorrie.

Dorrie's eyes flashed wide. "You mean that howling is coming from your dad?"

Mick nodded and gripped her hand as they walked down the carpeted hall together. Approaching the solarium where patients sat in wheelchairs watching television or catching a brief nap, Mick gestured her over to the far corner where a withered man lay howling in a lounge chair. Dorrie glanced up at Mick's face and saw the tears swimming in his eyes.

"It's okay, Mick," she whispered, squeezing his hand in reassurance.

"I. . .I don't know if I can take this, Dorrie," he whispered. "That. . .that stranger isn't my dad."

Just then they were interrupted by one of the nursing assistants on duty, who came over and introduced herself as Debbie. She recognized Mick at once and said hello.

"This is Dorrie," Mick said. "Dorrie, Debbie here takes care of Dad quite a bit."

"Hi, Debbie," Dorrie said brightly.

"Sorry, but your father is not in the greatest of moods today," Debbie sadly informed them. "He fought with me most of the day. I'm afraid we had to place him in a vest restraint for his safety."

"Vest restraint?" Dorrie wondered.

The pain in Mick's face was very evident as he choked out, "Yeah, sometimes when Dad is really off, he gets restless. The nurses are afraid he might fall and hurt himself. Sometimes they have to use the restraint."

Dorrie was shocked. "You mean they tie him in his chair? Oh Mick, that's awful!"

"It's only for his protection, miss," Debbie informed her. "Maybe if he calms down during your visit, we can take it off."

Dorrie swallowed hard. This was indeed worse than she

had imagined. The man she saw in the chair wore a simple patient's gown with an afghan draped over his lap. Spittle ran out of his mouth and down his neck. His gray eyes were glazed over as he stared into space. Dorrie tried to picture the man walking the streets of Boston, handing out tracts and telling others about the Lord. Her heart could not help but cry out for God's mercy to overshadow this pitiful man.

With great trepidation, Mick approached the bedraggled figure, knelt down next to the chair, and in a soft voice, greeted his father. Dorrie watched the interaction between father and son. She noticed the man move his eyes ever so slightly, followed by the loud word "eyow!"

Unprepared for the noise, Mick jumped to his feet. Trembling, he tried to regain his composure. "D. . .Dad, I want you to meet a friend of mine. This is Dorrie."

Dorrie stepped up and smiled down at the man. "Hello, Mr. Walters."

The man offered no response as he stared listlessly past her.

Dorrie drew in a breath, glancing at Mick for support. After an awkward moment, she decided to communicate with the man as if he could understand everything. Mick looked on as Dorrie explained who she was, where she worked, how she met Mick, and how she loved the Lord. At this, Mr. Walters swiveled his head slightly and emitted another ferocious "eyow!"

Dorrie's heart began to race with growing excitement. *I think Mick's mother is right! I think he does understand what I'm saying!* She then remembered the tract in her possession and withdrew it.

Upon seeing the familiar booklet in her outstretched hand, Mr. Walters strained against the restraint that held him in the chair and emitted another frightful "eyow." Everyone in the solarium glanced over in their direction. Some of the residents shouted at him to be quiet.

"What are you doing, Dorrie?" Mick scolded her. "You're getting him all upset."

"No, look again, Mick, and this time listen carefully to him." Once more, Dorrie showed him the tract and explained how Mick was thinking of going back out to the streets.

"Dorrie," Mick whispered furiously, "why did you tell him all that? He doesn't understand, I tell you."

"Look, Mick!" Dorrie exclaimed excitedly.

His father twisted and turned into contorted positions and yelled several additional "eyows" before he suddenly began to howl like an animal.

The nursing assistant rushed over to find out the reason for the commotion. "I'm afraid this visit is really upsetting him," Debbie observed in dissatisfaction. "Maybe you shouldn't talk to him but just sit quietly and hold his hand."

"No!" Dorrie fired back. "Debbie, this man knows what we're saying to him. Every time I mention something from his past, he says the word 'eyow.'" She turned to the man who now lay in the chair. "Isn't that true, Mr. Walters?"

Again, he roared an "eyow!"

"You see, you see?" Dorrie exclaimed in excitement, clutching Mick's arm. "That means, yes. Right, Mr. Walters?"

"Eyow!"

Mick and Debbie stared incredulously, first at the man and then at Dorrie. Now Dorrie knelt beside the man and pointed to the restraint. "I bet you dislike this thing, don't you, Mr. Walters?"

This sent the man into a fit along with more "eyows."

Mick needed no further convincing. "Take it off right now, Debbie," he ordered.

"I'm not sure if that's wise. . . ," the nursing assistant began.

"Take it off. If there's any chance at all my father understands what we're saying, then he must understand what is happening to him. Take it off now."

Debbie obliged to the echoes of "eyows" screeched by Mick's father.

"Let's roll him to his room where we can talk in private," Dorrie suggested.

Mick agreed, and together they steered the massive chair through the doors and down a hallway to his private room, overlooking the skyline of downtown Boston in the distance. Once in his room, Dorrie began to investigate the closet, searching for something to dress the man in besides the flimsy hospital gown. Finding no clothes in the closet, she asked Mick if his mother might consider bringing in some shirts and pants.

"Dorrie," he whispered, leading her by the arm over to one side of the room, "you can't dress him. He, well, he'll soil his clothes."

The comment sent his father into another wave of howls. Dorrie smiled when she heard the reaction. "You see, Mick? See how well your father can hear? And I tell you, he doesn't want to be dressed in an ugly old hospital gown. He wants to feel like a man again, don't you, Mr. Walters?"

"Eyow!" came the reply.

Dorrie went to the dresser and shuffled through bottles of aftershave and old toothbrushes until she found a comb. "Mick, how does your father wear his hair?"

"Parted on the side I think, uh, don't you, Dad?"

The man swiveled his head around and responded with the customary "eyow" for yes.

Dorrie combed out his hair, parted it to one side, then found a mirror so he might view his appearance. "How's that, Mr. Walters?"

"Eyow." He relaxed in his chair.

"You see, Mick? What did I tell you?" Dorrie then studied the man resting before her for several moments. Suddenly, as if the sun had risen, bringing light into the midst of darkness, she began to understand the poor man's plight. "I. . .I think I know what's going on inside you, Mr. Walters," she said softly. She knelt next to the chair, holding a bony hand in hers as she spoke directly to him. "You know everything that's going on. I don't think you've lost your thoughts or memories or ability to understand. What you lost is, well, like a road. . .a road linking thought with action. I've even heard about it. . . those people who have been in comas for years, then wake up and come to an understanding of what's happening around them. After extensive rehabilitation, they are able to talk about how their bodies were like shells, even prisons." Her grip strengthened around his withered hand. "Maybe you've even wondered. When, oh God, will someone realize I'm trapped in this body? I can think, I can feel, I can understand, but I can't tell anyone." Dorrie sniffed, overwhelmed by the words she spoke. "I want to tell people I'm alive, but this body is a prison with no way out."

At that moment, Dorrie saw a great tear fall from the man's eye and plop onto her arm. Mick saw it, too, and immediately came to his father's side, breaking down into tears. "I'm so sorry, Dad. I didn't understand. Mom. . .she believed. . .she believed you. I. . .I only wanted you back the way you used to be. I was mad at God and. . .and mad at you. Please. . .forgive me for abandoning you, for not caring, for not being there when you needed me most."

Again, another tear slipped out of the man's eyes. "Eyow, eyow, eyow," he cried, along with the weeping pair next to him. No one knew the thoughts circulating in the head of the street preacher at that moment of triumph. *Oh God, at last, at last,* his mind cried. *Thank you for restoring me to my son. Thank you for my family, for through this angel of mercy which You gave understanding to, I can now be understood by my son. Thank you merciful God.*

fifteen

Mick did not want to leave his father's side but reluctantly bid his father good-bye, accompanied by a kiss on the forehead. He then told him about the picnic Mom had planned at a nearby park. "Wish he could come with us," Mick said to Dorrie as they found their way out of the brick building and into the sunshine that glowed even more brilliantly after the visit.

"There's no reason why he can't learn to sit in a wheelchair so you can take him out places. It looks like that nurse, Debbie, is a blessing. She seemed quite open to hearing new ideas on how to care for your father. She's willing to dress him in decent clothes using those adult pads and everything. This is a new day in his life."

"It's a new day in all our lives. I can't wait to tell Mom. She'll be so excited to hear this. Mom has spent nearly every waking hour of her life with Dad. I know she'll be glad to hear that I now understand what's going on and that Dad does, too."

"It will be a wonderful surprise for her," Dorrie agreed.

The park on the other side of town was crowded with members of Mick's congregation, who had gathered together for a Columbus Day picnic. Grills were fired up, ready for one final barbecue before winter settled in over the New England city. Checkered tablecloths, lying across the picnic tables, fluttered in the autumn breeze. When Mick and Dorrie arrived, Mrs. Walters came over to greet them. She was a tall woman with chestnut brown hair, bobbed in a style similar to what Dorrie wore before her accident on Mount Washington.

Dorrie sensed an immediate bonding with the woman as Mrs. Walters bestowed a warm hug, thanking Dorrie for all she had done.

"You won't believe our visit at the nursing home, Mom," Mick said, eagerly filling her in on the restoration between himself and his father that afternoon. As he spoke, a small crowd from the church gathered around to hear the story, then exchanged hugs with an exuberant Mrs. Walters.

Tears of joy ran down her cheeks. "Oh, Mick, how I've prayed that one day you would understand your father and how much he loves you. I'm so glad!"

"I would have never understood, Mom," Mick said slowly, turning toward Dorrie, "if it had not been for this terrific lady here."

"How can I ever thank you, Dorrie? You've been such a blessing to me and my family."

Dorrie only smiled, embarrassed by all the attention she was receiving from the people around her. "I'm just glad for you," she managed to say.

Mick wrapped his arm around her and gave her an affectionate squeeze. "She's been a godsend to me, Mom," he agreed.

"She's definitely an answer to a prayer," Mrs. Walters added with a twinkle in her eye. "Well, Dorrie, you must be hungry. Come, there're hamburgers ready."

Dorrie eagerly helped herself to the food, then became immersed in conversation as people inquired of her escapades in the mountains. After it was all over, Dorrie collapsed inside Mick's car, spent from all the flurry of activity and the emotion of the day. "Wow, I'm bushed!"

"Me, too."

"What a great day. You have two wonderful families, Mick—your real family and your church family."

"I have wonderful friends, too, Dorrie," he added with a

sideways glance toward her.

Dorrie looked over at him and considered his words. Somehow, after the events of the day, the word "friend" did not seem to fit Mick Walters anymore. What was he, then, if he was not a friend? He was not a brother, of course. Was he someone else. . .a special someone that now began to tug on her heart?

The two of them spent Sunday once more surrounded by Mick's two families and also visited Mick's dad at the nursing home for a lengthy time, sharing Scriptures and the message from the pulpit that morning. The nurses remarked how calm Mr. Walters had become since their previous visit and marveled at his transformation. Debbie had him dressed in some of his regular clothes with his hair parted to one side. Both Mick and Dorrie sensed that dignity and hope had been restored to the man who once gave everything in his life to others less fortunate.

"He looked real good," Mick commented over a steak dinner in a fancy restaurant that night—his going-away present to Dorrie before she was obliged to leave early for New York the next morning. "This has been quite a weekend."

"Yes," she agreed, stirring a packet of artificial sweetener into her iced tea.

Mick stared at her thoughtfully, then inquired if she was looking forward to seeing New York.

Dorrie shrugged, growing suddenly despondent with the thought of returning home.

"Well, I have something for you," Mick told her with a mysterious look in his eye.

A strange fear welled up inside her until he handed her a clear plastic egg. She stared at it in confusion. "What is this?"

"Got it out of one of those quarter machines the other day," he told her as she opened the egg to reveal a plastic ring. He added quickly, "Thought it would make a good friendship ring."

Dorrie snickered, shaking her head at him. "How silly."

"Well, I wanted to give you a souvenir rock from Mount Washington, but I figured that wouldn't go over too well." He returned his attention to the healthy-size portion of steak on a stone platter in front of him.

Dorrie eyed the ring as she twisted it around her finger. A strange sensation swept over her. When she glanced up to see Mick busily chewing his meal, his blue eyes twinkling, she knew what the sensation was that now fell on her like a gentle rain. It was love, pure and simple. Dorrie knew without a doubt she was in love with the man sitting before her.

After dinner, Mick dropped her off at the motel. "I'll come by early to see you off," he promised before returning to his car.

"Okay." Dorrie closed the door to her motel room, then withdrew the ring from her purse. Did this ring speak of a friendship or a longing for a deeper commitment? Dorrie relaxed on the bed, thinking of the exciting things that had happened over the course of her stay in Boston. She remembered how the eyes of Mr. Walters shone when Mick discussed his plan to return to the streets of Boston and share the gospel with those in need. Truly Mick had become a changed man—one who now looked heavenward to the eternal things of the Lord rather than the carnal things of this world. How different he had become since that night on the trail after her ankle injury. How different she had become during these last few days. Dorrie felt her reservations slowly melt away as her questions were replaced by an assurance that this was indeed God's will at work in their lives.

The following morning Mick arrived as promised with bagels, cream cheese, and juice for a quick breakfast. Dorrie could barely spread the cheese on a bagel. Her heart overflowed with a love that seemed to affect her in everything she did, from packing her suitcase to brushing her teeth to eating the food he had lovingly brought. Now she set the bagel down and closed her eyes.

Mick noticed her lack of appetite right away. His gentle eyes narrowed in concern. "Did I get the wrong kind of bagels? Maybe I should've asked you what flavor you like."

Suddenly Dorrie burst into tears. Mick sat stunned, holding a bagel in one hand. Quickly he placed it on a napkin and sat beside her. "Dorrie, what's the matter?"

Unable to bear it anymore, she turned and threw her arms around him. "I love you, Mick!"

"Dorrie. . . ," he began, slowly allowing his arms to enfold her in an embrace.

"I'm sorry it took me so long to see." She laughed a little. "Guess the bump on my head up there in the mountain did something to my vision. I could not even see the terrific guy sitting right underneath my nose."

Mick could only smile and thank God in his heart for this revelation.

Dorrie turned, zipped open her purse, and handed him the plastic ring.

"Would you like to exchange this for a real one, instead?" he asked her softly.

Dorrie nodded. "Yes!" she breathed. Mick bent over her and their lips met in a passionate kiss as a signature of their commitment to one another. When they parted, Dorrie clung to his arm as if she never wanted to let go. She praised God that indeed He had purified their hearts and their very being in the great and awesome majesty of His mountains. Soon He would bring them together as one in the high and holy calling of the marriage covenant.

A Letter To Our Readers

Dear Reader:

In order that we might better contribute to your reading enjoyment, we would appreciate your taking a few minutes to respond to the following questions. When completed, please return to the following:

Rebecca Germany, Managing Editor
Heartsong Presents
P.O. Box 719
Uhrichsville, Ohio 44683

1. Did you enjoy reading *Mountaintop?*
   - ❑ Very much. I would like to see more books
     by this author!
   - ❑ Moderately
     I would have enjoyed it more if _____

   _____

2. Are you a member of **Heartsong Presents**? ❑Yes ❑No
   If no, where did you purchase this book?_____

   _____

3. What influenced your decision to purchase this
   book? (Check those that apply.)

❑ Cover	❑ Back cover copy
❑ Title	❑ Friends
❑ Publicity	❑ Other_____

4. How would you rate, on a scale from 1 (poor) to 5
   (superior), the cover design?_____

5. On a scale from 1 (poor) to 10 (superior), please rate the following elements.

    __Heroine   __Plot

    __Hero   __Inspirational theme

    __Setting   __Secondary characters

6. What settings would you like to see covered in **Heartsong Presents** books?_____

_____

_____

7. What are some inspirational themes you would like to see treated in future books?_____

_____

_____

8. Would you be interested in reading other **Heartsong Presents** titles? ❑ Yes   ❑ No

9. Please check your age range:
    ❑ Under 18   ❑ 18-24   ❑ 25-34
    ❑ 35-45   ❑ 46-55   ❑ Over 55

10. How many hours per week do you read? _____

Name _____

Occupation _____

Address _____

City _____ State _____ Zip _____

Christmas Dreams

*Four new inspirational love stories
from Christmas present*

Evergreen by Rebecca Germany
To fill the void of her first holiday alone, Nora agrees to do a newspaper story on the homeless shelters—accompanied by a certain rakishly handsome photographer.

Search for the Star by Mary Hawkins
To Jean Drew, Christmas in Australia is a time to work, until this year, when she is invited to witness her niece's wedding and meets a man from her past who once embodied all of Jean's dreams.

The Christmas Wreath by Veda Boyd Jones
Mike Shannon is seeking peace and quiet this Christmas, but he finds neither when he encounters the woman of his dreams.

Christmas Baby by Melanie Panagiotopoulos
Christmas amid the ruins in Athens, Greece, on the arm of a modern-day Adonis, sounds like a dream vacation. But there's a much more poignant reason for Christina's visit. . .her birth mother.

(352 pages, Paperbound, 5" x 8")

Heartsong

HEARTSONG PRESENTS *TITLES AVAILABLE NOW:*